First Edition

Cover illustration by Luis Méndez Rock, visit him here:
www.madriphur.org

Visit the author, Antwel T. Higgins, here:
www.instagram.com/antwel.higgins/

Contents:

To, Auntie Donna

"They say the Lion and the Lizard keep
The Courts where Jamshyd gloried and drank deep;
    And Bahram, that great Hunter—the Wild Ass
Stamps o'er his Head, and he lies fast asleep."

—The Rubaiyat of Omar Khayyam: XVIII

Arthur

LARRY THE LIZARD
BOOK ONE: THE PATH OF BONE

PART I

Larry smiled wide and showed all of his teeth. Larry was a good liar; he hid well what he was. "So, you enjoyed the drive, Mrs.?" Larry asked the woman he had steadily sought to hypnotise with the swirling yellows of his eyes.

"Yes!" she returned a reply, quite slow, half distracted, moving then to ask, "Why, kids, what did you think?"

"Balloons, mummy, balloons!" cried three children, tugging at their mother's long, white skirt.

"That's right," said Larry. "Mummy and I made a promise, and a promise we'll keep, for you were all so well behaved and good in the car for mummy and me. So here you go, my sweet things. Now sit, and play nicely and make not a single peep," finished Larry, handing out six balloons, one for each the children's hands, and turning to their mother, smiling quite brilliant, quite widely, he spoke softly and beckoned directly into mummy's left ear: "So, Mrs., what says you? shall we talk numbers alone, just for a few?"

The woman took Larry by his outstretched arm, she nodded, her eyes grew wide and expectant and under a redness and subtle heaviness somewhat sleepy, somewhat dazed. Into his office they left and they vanished. The door was closed and business thought to be discussed as frequent laughing was heard by the children whom outside sat and waited, overcome with a will to sit and be good. A voice was once raised and loud, long gasps came following, one bemused moan, one frightened grunt, and a chair went falling, and then all was still, all remained silent for sometime and a while.

Three balloons had popped of their own accord, their own fickle nature, by when Larry and mummy had finished with their business; and for the three balloons left intact they hung like frowning, sad faces, like heads decomposed, skulls grown soft, caved, crumpled and sunken.

There was no burst of excitement from the children when finally their mummy reappeared, no stir, no movement, even when Larry came rushing, came crying, came laughing, "There they are, there's the little monsters!" his hands held aloft like pretend, make-believe pinchers. Larry groped and he grabbed of the children's faces three lethargic, strained smiles both at once unamused and fearfully bewildered.

#

Midnight neared, like a long awaited taxi, and Larry took leave of the car showroom. He always stayed behind after everyone else. His boss liked it, seemed to think Larry was somehow doing him good; that was just the impression Larry gave him, however. Larry wasn't working, or doing good. Larry was drinking.

Truth is, Larry couldn't quite face leaving the showroom until darkness had for a time settled and all about the night was vacant and still; dead and silent. He didn't want to be spotted, you see. For when he took off his face, he was quite sure he'd be seen.

It wasn't until around midnight that usually found he arrived the comfortable darkness and quiet of the night, usually felt he tipsy enough to wobble out his office door, out the showroom and drop the smile he'd carried all day. Such a weight on his face. He never knew when he'd be spotted; so, he wore his smile behind his office door; wore it in the toilets, even the toilet cubicles; wore it when they weren't looking, to be sure they wouldn't ever see.

He'd drop the grin he'd worn all day the second he stepped off the showroom lot. Drop it on the side of the street, like a mucky old rag, where he would find it again early next morn and wipe it clean of the grime overnight there it would have collected; scales each day he polished, scales that looked to the passing eye or content gaze like the ordinary grin of a one happy and benign, smiling Larry.

Larry slunk into the darkness, and under the silver moonlight he felt at peace. Quietude filled him, and burned he inside with an itch: the eternal desire for another drink. Maybe a few drinks, maybe another mummy, he thought to himself as insidious laughter, *delight*, climbed up, climbed out his throat; and his scales shone in the moon's coldness; Her glimmering light.

Larry crawled into the damp air of a midnight tavern, unnoticed by its occupants (unnoticed, even, as he set his claws down across the bar and perched his large boned behind on an iron stool), and he began to fill the quietly cackling hole of his face with a strong spirit.

Whisky was his drink. The barman hadn't even noticed Larry when he poured the first glass for him, or when Larry took the bottle himself. Just a dark figure poking money out of shadows, dark, quiet and laughing.

Who's sobbing? the barman thought once looking in Larry's direction, but the thought seemed to crumple in his mind and he threw it away with a shudder, for Larry turned silent then and with a dim glare of his yellow eyes peaked from out the darkness and obscured the barman's thought.

Larry was the last man still drinking when dawn's first light dimmed the night sky. Even the barman had left! Larry swung open the tavern door, disappointed to greet the shrinking darkness of night-time quietude, and his eyes, how he had to recoil and hide behind his arm for a moment;—the first slithers of morning light always stung him the most.

When finally he could again see, his eyes readjusted, the slits they had been in the dark as he'd squinted over drink after drink and glared frequently, unseen at the flesh of bodies that had been about him, suddenly, his eyes once slits were now round and friendly: agleam with shimmering points of a fine light.

He breathed in remnant wisps of the night's silent air and walked cautiously, in the growing light of morn, pertaining to shadowed recesses, down streets, along a string of allies, round many a bend, and, finally, to the curb outside his car showroom.

He had returned to the curb whilst light was still dark enough, streets quiet enough, that for moments he was safe from the sight of eyes. His smile was still there. Right where he'd left it, on the floor, by his feet. He picked it up and tied it around his head. The miserable moan of exposed fangs hidden, pulled tight, wide, readjusted.

The boss approached him from behind; the day grew brighter.

"Nice and early, Larry, as always," said the boss with authentic rings of cheer to each word and syllable.

"Yes," said Larry, "you know me." Goosebumps flickered across Larry's scaled flesh, and he thought about slitting the boss's throat right there whilst the morning was quiet, and of draining his blood into the curb-side gutter.

Larry walked the path to the showroom's front doors slowly, allowing the boss to walk before him, so that Larry could, privily, gaze at his phone; and what a joy it brought to see: Larry had missed calls, voicemails, and a list of text messages. It was the woman from yesterday, the one he'd let drive him around town, the one with three kids. "Hello mummy," said Larry behind the toothy grin of a wide smile. She was coming back, and today. She was doing as he'd told and leaving the children home alone.

Larry stepped inside the showroom and slunk across the polished floors before the boss could think to make a further polite and unwanted conversation. Larry went into his office and locked the door. He kept his smile on and in place, tightly alert and stretched across his face, as better it was he not touch the scales of his grin whilst he worked, not loosen or alter its grip whilst the sun still shone, whilst there was pollen yet to collect, and on this day, four persons; one big and three little, to deceive.

He took off his belt and pulled down his trousers, then his pants, and sat back in his chair. He began to listen to mummy's voicemails. The blinds were positioned at an angle so that his office was cast in a semi-darkness. Just how Larry liked it.

He could see you, but you wouldn't see him.

#

Larry had managed to seduce her enough in the office the day before. The short fumble they'd had. The slight struggle she'd put up. She hadn't struggled long. She hadn't struggled at all when Larry got her by the eyes.

The voicemails were delicious. Larry enjoyed this part of his work. The seduction. The theft of another's senses; nobility. (It was like wine to him. And it was easy. Like the hypnotising of cattle, wooing of lustful maidens.) Docile idiots, Larry thought, and smiled, contemptuously, *mentally unfit, sensually distractible, sloths and whores, the lot of them.* Larry was feeling rather like a sheep dog as he sat in his chair, his flesh excited between his legs, in fact, he was panting like a sheep dog; long and narrow tongue lolling out a gap in his smiling fangs; that was when his friend had almost arrived and she sent him another text:

'I'm almost there, Larry! I've been thinking about you all night.'

Larry got up, leaving his trousers and pants on the floor beneath his desk, and walked, naked but for his shirt and tie and a grey blazer that nobody ever seemed to notice the layers of dirt upon, or reek of spirits, or spots of blood, toward his office door. He unlocked it, remained smiling in the dark for a few moments, and then peered at his phone, and, with delighted thumbs, typed his friend a reply:

'My door's unlocked, mummy. Come right on in.'

Larry sat back in his office chair, put his arms behind his head and relaxed in the cool dark. Shortly then, he saw a figure approaching through the blinds, the door handle begin to turn, and the door, only a crack at first, open, then quarter way it slowly swung and in someone slid. Larry tilted back his head and sniffed the air, invitingly. The door closed.

"You smell nice," whispered Larry through grinning teeth. "Please, mummy, turn on the light and take a seat. The switch is to your left." On she turned the light, and Larry saw her: she wore a dark red dress and it clung to her; none of her was kept from the mind, all of her was offered to the sight, even her nipples were showing for the tightness of the dress and absence of a brassiere. This is much unlike her, Larry thought, delighted and growing hot. Yesterday it was a white scarf, long, white skirt and a green cardigan buttoned high.

"So, how can daddy help?"

"Well, I was hoping we could talk about that car again?" she said, her eyes averting to the floor.

Ssss, she's going to fly. The blast car? "I see, mummy," Larry said slowly and with a husk, reaching across the table to snare her hand in his as tried he to catch her eyes in a gaze she would not escape. But she moved backward in her seat, and Larry saw that she was beyond a mere state of discomfort; she was starting to panic.

She began feeling at her dress, seeming to grow at once embarrassed in the tightness of it. She stood. She looked down at herself. The next words to come out of her mouth were lost in a quiet scream as Larry got up from behind his desk and swiftly moved toward her. She had become disillusioned. And if Larry hadn't made for her so, and quickly, if he hadn't grabbed her and covered with a large and scaly hand her lipstick smothered lips, why, she would have surely given him away, and that would have provided Larry with quite some unfortunate circumstance (but nothing that Larry hasn't handled before).

The quiet scream Larry managed to catch and cup in one large claw before she erupted into hysterics was less than likely due to the lower nudity of her car salesman; and more than likely to have been at the colour of Larry's scaled skin. You see, if you haven't guessed by now, Larry isn't human. He isn't even close.

Larry's a lizard.

Those that see Larry for what he actually is don't usually look again, or they wait too long to look and Larry is gone. Larry knows when you've seen him, or when it is that you're about to see.

The woman struggled in Larry's strong grasp. She struggled to breathe, struggled to break free. Larry stared into her eyes from over her left shoulder. She couldn't help but stare back, and slowly, she was drawn into his gaze and Larry's scents filled her nostrils, and when next she noticed Larry's smile hanging over her her eyes had softened and her arms rose upward to wrap around his neck, and she embraced him.

"Oh, Larry," she said, "take me on your desk. I've been a naughty mummy, Larry. I left my kids at home, like you asked, and I'm not wearing panties. Take me. Take me." She stroked his slimy face with one hand and stared into his yellow, swirling eyes. *Yes mummy, I'll take you, and I'll abduct your children when I'm done. My wife grows hungry. They'll buy me a week, each one of them.*

Larry twirled around beneath the bright lights of his office with the woman tightly netted in his arms. Then he threw her down onto his desk. He locked the door. Between his legs his flesh pulsed and grew with excitement, his tongue came poking out a gap in his fangs, and when he took her, to her surprise, he smiled wide and consumed her one bite at a time.

#

Larry bagged her up. She fit nicely. That's right, beware any rainbows in this tale. Larry has spent the last hour chewing through joints and ligaments. Her clothes he's put in a desk drawer: he will sniff them while he drinks, later tonight. He enjoyed reminiscing over the women, or the men, that he seduced. Somehow, they felt like partners to him, friends for the briefest of time, companions in a joy all his—his for the devouring. Their clothes were the only mementos of a job well done, of the delicious taste they afforded him, the joy that was, as he ruled over them, his.

But Larry in truth was a sad, sad lizard at heart. A sympathetic mind might presume to say that that was why Larry did what he did; for he suffered beneath the weight and torture of his own loneliness. (But why he lived in the dark and clawed out of shadow for the touch and the taste of flesh was not to be so easily summed up; like I have said to you, Larry is not made in the image you and I are, and you have not heard the rest of Larry's tale yet. I could sum it up for you. Maybe you don't want to read on? maybe what you have found out about Larry has disturbed you enough already;—so, suppose I, for those of you who would duck and dive, I will say this: if ever there was a wife who's mirth was the evil of her husband, it was Larry's; if ever there was a man who would rather chow down on a corpse than be close to his wife, it was Larry.)

In the bright lighting of his office Larry placed her, limb by limb, into an old and tattered, black satin sack that had carried many for the same purpose. "Nectar in a bag," Larry mumbled to himself, the fun having shrunk from his game as much as it had in his pants, and as much as the taste of her flesh was gone from his lips and his stomach felt very full.

Her home was most impressive when he arrived. Larry had made sure to get the address out of her before she'd been driven numb under the operative strokes of his claws; once she had become numb with desire for Larry however, she had spoke quite freely and often about all things she held dear. And she really had left the kids at home like Larry asked. No babysitter, either. No dogs, or security. She had probably spent the whole night staring into her bathroom mirror, watching her eyes as Larry's reflection glimmered back and her hands wandered to squeeze and play with the carnal stirrings in the flesh. Lust was easy for Larry to excite. Larry sniggered at the thought of his image present to his victim. He was observing in the woman's ensuite bathroom an image quite like a demon, quite like a lizard, drawn in lipstick, upon a mirror's surface. So many times Larry had seen his own portrait like this, and still he could not but ponder (still, it made him laugh).

He had arrived with balloons and told the children that their mummy sent him. They were easily tricked.

Two boys and one girl. The girl, slightly older yet just as malleable as the boys, seemed for a moment to raise her eyebrows in distrust at Larry's proposal that they follow him to meet mummy. He had even thought, for a daunting second, that she was going to ask what was in the sack over Larry's back. But she didn't, none of them so much as questioned him when he brought out the balloons and mentioned in a loud and entreating voice, "Ice cream and candy." (He hadn't even knocked on the front door; he'd just crept in, and appeared to them in the kitchen. That was one of Larry's ways.)

Down cobbled streets they tottered, their mummy all chewed and chopped into pieces, chunks of flesh scattered like crumbs over four dead limbs, a head and a torso, all neatly hidden in Larry's old sack. Halfway there and the boys were fighting over balloons, the girl stuck in the middle and not helping. Halfway there and the sharp glints in Larry's eyes were blinding people as they walked by.

Nobody would think to stop them, nobody would have a chance to look twice; for if anyone saw Larry's appearance, and it unnerved them, threw up a question to their mind, well, Larry would get a tingling sensation, and he'd turn a corner before they again looked; and if it was they remembered what they'd seen, remembered the green and the scales, the toothy, fanged grin, they'd doubt it in their minds later! Larry sensed the alertness and directive of people, it was all he cared for.

Larry's wife was waiting at home, and Larry was confident, happy, he had all the pollen she would need for near a month.

Up tall and winding steps the children skipped and jumped. Larry lugging behind the weight of their mother. One of them looked back however, and all three began to cry. Larry apologised quickly and promised in a hissing voice that at the very top of the building, behind a door at the end of a corridor: "Are lots and lots of ice cream and mummy waiting with smiles and laughs."

The two boys and the girl then ran, and skipped, and jumped up the stairs, and chased each other down a long and brightly lit corridor to the door of Larry's wife's abode. They tried the handle and barked with glee for mummy to answer. But they had to wait, for Larry trailed behind carrying a large sack in which mummy was slung right over his back. Larry put his key in the door, turned the lock, and down the children pulled on the handle. In they fell, two boys, one girl, into a trap they never could have foreseen or foretold.

They entered the flat, a stinky abode they'd never before been, at the top of a tall and grey building, without a question to their wits. They'd barely noticed where they were until the room into which they fell was so dimly lit, the wallpaper a muddy brown and the carpet a slimy green, that they suddenly felt afraid. "I don't like it," the girl began to cry. But the boys, why, seeing their sister's tears, laughed and were more than pleased to jump on a couch, point, giggle, kick at the air and fall down, sinking into old leather still wet with someone's awful sweat.

Larry's wife came shortly onto the scene. (This is when Larry emptied their mummy out of the sack and onto the carpet.)

"There, there, my sweet ones," came a voice from shadows, delicate and deep. "It's okay now. That's not your mummy. Not really." Large, much larger than Larry, was Larry's wife; a great bulbous mass of shadow, a black, black fright. Her face was so terrible it is a blessing that all here there is to say is that shadow covered all, shadows swarming against walls. The children in weeping screamed and ran blindly into the reaching arms come from darkness to soothe and love.

The room fell silent. Not a whisper, nor a squeak. The children curled into tiny balls of shadow beneath Larry's wife who said nothing more but *hushed* and *cooed*; Larry knew to leave. And so he did, he left and he locked the door; left his daemon wife to feed.

#

Dusk was passing when Larry returned to the showroom. The front door was locked. Larry used his own personal set of keys to let himself in. Larry was like that, having his own personal set of keys to the workplace where he wasn't the boss; heck, Larry had the keys to his wife's health and future, but he was not in charge of her (not a smidge). Larry allowed you all the illusions that you so desired, so long as it meant that he got what *he* so wanted, that you didn't see through his smile, or look away from the swirling yellows of his eyes when he lent in to seduce.

Larry was having coitus with his victims long before they'd ever thought of letting him pull down their pants. The moment those eyes, swirling, glinting, slanted lizard eyes stared into yours, you were in a bed, in your mind's eye, Larry's scaly hands greeting your flesh.

Larry's eyes merely blinded you for a moment's intervention, if you weren't susceptible to his trickery; a hideous truth, blaring light, lanced, thrust into your depth, flickered and was gone. You saw something pass you. A man in a dirty grey blazer, with green skin, and yellow eyes.

"It was a migraine, mild hallucination," your doctor tells you. Your trust keeps you sane; the doctor might put you on medication.

Larry collected mummy's dress now, out his draw where he had placed it. He stroked it in his lap as he sat in his office chair. He could feel her skin in his mind when he touched it. Her smell was still in his nostrils. He wasn't going to ruin the fabric, yet. He would wait to ravage the scents of her perfume and body from the fibres of the dress once he'd walked his delighted stroll under moonlight, contently drunk with Her silver rays. And then, from a lone seat in a tavern he would seep through his pores the smell of mummy's flesh, her pheromones, fresh in the netting fibres of her dark red dress.

Midnight came and Larry left the showroom. The moon was large and beaming Her silver rays across the sky. Larry stopped before he stepped out into Her light. He thought about the children. Three feedings they had bought him. Three feedings and three weeks to himself.

His wife fed on them, the children, by hushing their fears, making them hers. She hushed and cooed until they fell asleep. For three weeks she would mother them, until the shadow swells over the walls and her other children accept the rascals. Larry wouldn't see their faces the next time he crept by, for they'd be consumed by then, the darkness of his wife's abode a little denser.

Larry strolled and the moon's rays rolled across his skin; and his scales shone like silver fire across green skin, luminous and dazzling. On nights like this Larry was most happy, he felt like his joy would never end.

#

Yellow and swirling, glinting spirals of light; his eyes stared up while he stared down. A glass empty of the spirit he drank, Larry stared into his eyes in the reflection of his glass. He stared content, ablaze with pangs of joy. The tavern that in he chose to sit, far past the stroke of midnight's tick, was filled with bodies, people infatuated and mesmerised, drawn like bugs around the flickering of a pleasant, bright light; (only the light in their tavern was a hide, and that hide was Larry's, his scales teeming, brimming with retained streams of the moon's silver light).

Larry sat on a lone stool centre to the bar, clothed in not shadow, hidden in no darkness, shielded without grin; silver fires raged across his scaled skin. Around him the warm bodies danced, bumped, rubbed, wobbled on drunken knees, caressed and squeezed, kissed and sucked, and Larry, agleam, emitting a silver light that intoxicated the whole scene, cared nothing for the herd mesmerised and filling one of his taverns to the very seams. Larry but stared into the glass; his yellow, swirling eyes, glinting spirals of light;

they stared up, while he stared down.

PART II

Larry the Lizard dragged his cargo down an unlit alley. The sky above was a cold sea of roving black forms absent the light of the moon, stars shone bleakly through a pale mist that had formed over the night, and Larry's cargo was coming awake. Larry, however, had tied tight a gag about the mouth of his cargo: a man whom severely had wronged him—or, more importantly, as Larry feared, put a price on his head. There was nothing he could see, the man Larry dragged, no inch in which he would find escape at the end of Larry's rope as he began to wriggle and squirm. Larry had wrapped his cargo in black satin, head-to-toe, that they not be easily spotted.

Ahead, a manhole cover lay beneath the glare of four cul-de-sac streetlamps. There was no choice for Larry but to enter the streetlight and risk being seen.

Larry pulled the heavily breathing, struggling man wrapped in black satin to the edge of the alley, edge of darkness. Larry left him there and ran with rope in hand toward the manhole cover. The lid Larry tore away at once like a sheet of paper. His claws, black like obsidian, glinted with the orange hue of streetlamp light as he pulled hurriedly by rope the satin bound man toward the open sewer. He slung the man over one shoulder and stabbed him with his left claw that he stop his struggling and remain quiet as, for a moment, Larry paused to listen.

The night was silent, no shadows or footsteps lurked in any hidden corner, no eyes itched Larry with their gaze. All was dead of the night, but for the one owl that screeched and stared from ahigh the branch of a sycamore tree, with bright magma-orange eyes, as Larry climbed into the sewer and reached out with one green, scaled hand to pull back in-place the manhole cover.

#

It was early in the morning and sunlight meekly invaded the night from the outer ridge of the horizon; so that all contained beneath the night's blanket slept soundly that slept and stirred not before the coming presence of morn's light. And it was this morning of which I speak that Larry, wide awake as ever he was upon the utmost rim of night, stared with mesmerised eyes into the shallow black pool of spirit at the bottom of his whiskey glass; this morning, as sunlight flooded the tavern in Larry sat, he did not realise, would not know for until almost three weeks had passed, that a loose end was arriving home from business out of town to find missing and absent both children and wife.

As Larry got up from his barstool, walked over the bodies that around him lie, Larry was oblivious to the fact that halfway across town a man had arrived home and seen Larry's picture drawn by his wife. Larry's face was still unknown to the man however, for the image he found spoke more of madness than anything else; for what he had seen was either a daemon or lizard, drawn upon his wife's bathroom mirror in lines of red lipstick, and held no clue to his mind of who, what or where may have taken or seen his wife and children go.

Larry took leave of the tavern to stroll beneath a dark blue sky. In his left hand he carried a red dress, a dress he had sniffed most the night, a dress that belonged to no other than this man's wife. Larry was quite content still from the lustful seduction, meal and dismemberment of that women whom the red dress had belonged. He was rather still quite happy for having delivered her three children to his despicable wife; content was Larry that morn as he walked beneath the shrinking of the night sky.

Larry returned this day outside his place of work before the light upon the outer ridge of the sky had invaded far enough to sting and hurt his eyes. Larry picked from the floor the mask that he wore, the smile he tied each day around his green, scaled lizard face, and he walked toward the car showroom and unlocked the front door. Larry would catch some sleep before he started the day. Larry would need some sleep, as he hadn't slept yesterday; no, his brief visit with a mummy of three early that morn had seen to that.

Larry locked his office door, placed the red dress back in one of his draws and fell asleep strewn across the floor. The man across town wailed his wife's name, moaned for his two boys and one girl. (The man across town would not find proper rest for nearly a whole week.)

#

"WHO ARE YOU?" Larry blurted into a mirror's dimly lit reflection in an apartment that was not his. "Who are you?" he asked again. Larry had been staring into his own eyes, contented, as his gaze had swirled before him, the deep yellows of his eyes glinting, and he had lost himself. Larry only realised then how long he had been staring, when the sunlight broke through a parting between drawn curtains and struck the mirror's surface. "Who are you? You in those eyes, glinting, glimmering, shimmering—hypnotising I?! What magic is this that mine own eyes stare at me with; HOW LONG have I been here?" Larry breathed hard as his claws pressed into the mirror: the glass cracked, shattered. Larry turned, walking away.

He knew of the time that had slipped by; he knew it had been almost a full day since first he peered into his own bewildering gaze.

Larry left the scene with a victim slung over his back. He locked the apartment door and hurried.

23

#

Larry's loss of time scared him, and the power that he begot by the swirling allure of his eyes he became curious of. A great deal of time he spent staring into his reflection when time was spare and he found himself alone. He questioned with his gaze the power that resided therein, the light that entranced even him. Larry found his questioning to be of no avail and his staring into the swirling patterns of his eyes only to procure him with headaches. It had been almost three weeks since Larry had brought to his wife a child, when he was spied one night disposing of a woman from out his black satin sack.

As Larry was emptying (the parts he would not eat; breasts, face, feet and hands) a green-eyed victim into a river, beneath a bridge, that often he visited for such this purpose, Larry felt a pair of eyes itching his side when he reemerged out of darkness, into streetlight.

Without so much as giving hint to the discovery of his watcher, Larry continued to stroll along shadowed paths. Larry did not know who was following him. He was aware, however, that his activities sometimes drew unwanted attention.

Larry was heading back to the woman's apartment whom he had last devoured. The man following Larry was armed. Larry smiled a lascivious smile. Another meal, he thought as he strolled back to the dead women's apartment, confident that the man following would not be adequately armed to deal with the surprise of Larry; the strength and cunning of Larry;

or Larry's seduction. Larry chuckled to himself at these thoughts.

A torrent of rain poured from the skies as Larry arrived back at a block of apartments. Larry had kept the gaze of his stalker close by, so as not to lose him through the darkness of the night. And when Larry entered the apartments, he paused briefly in the dense rain and looked over his shoulder and then hurried inside and scuttled quickly up a flight of stairs. He opened the apartment door with the woman's key, and he waited to hear his stalker enter the building, and when the man following him was inside, Larry slunk into the apartment and slammed the door shut.

In the darkness Larry hid and he waited. The man following made his way up the flight of stairs.

The door handle turned. Larry smiled in the dark, a broad, toothy smile full of fangs. Open swung the door. In the man walked. The man who had finally tracked Larry down. The man was standing in the centre of the apartment now, a blood soaked bed against one wall, drawn curtains before him, and Larry hidden somewhere in the encircling dark. The man was armed, he wielded a large hatchet. He smelled of booze. Larry sniffed the air. The man turned and he faced the dark that concealed Larry the Lizard.

Larry opened wide his bright yellow eyes from the slits through which he had been peeking, and the man gasped and staggered back. "Daemon!" cried the man, and Larry stood tall and stepped forward. The man shrunk at the enormous height of Larry (and such a height it was when he was not crouched or skulking); Larry towered over the man, his yellow eyes beaming down, enormous and glowing. The man dropped the hatchet. Larry raised one claw to lift the man by his brown jacket.

"Who are you?" hissed Larry.

"I—I—" stuttered the man, "I'm her husband. You gave my children to a beast, and you kept my wife for yourself." The man struggled weakly in Larry's grasp, his eyes drawn into Larry's gaze; bravely, he fought to look away, and (upon managing to break contact for the briefest of seconds with the swirling yellows of Larry's eyes) he said in a sobbing cackle: "The beast, I have slain."

Larry strained his eyes wide and he brought the man's face close to his fangs, and said, in a cold whisper, "*Good.*"

#

Whence Larry came the wife was sacred, the wife was a Goddess; and Larry had allowed her blood to be spilt.

Larry kept the man whom had spilt his wife's blood bound and gagged at the women's apartment he had last devoured, and he made his way to his wife's abode atop a grey and unfriendly block of flats. All the while Larry could not help but feel pleased: she was dead. No longer was he bound by her need; no longer would he be her servant. He returned only to dispose of her body and to pocket her black heart.

Larry had to make sure he recovered his wife's heart. For if he did not, if the pearl of her decadence weren't extracted, why, whomsoever wished to seek the dimension of Larry would have themselves a key, and all next they would require is a gate.

The door to his wife's flat was open. No other apartment dwelt on the uppermost floor of the grey block of flats; and this is a fortunate fact, because if they had, Larry would have found it near impossible to retrieve her heart, having if the police had gotten involved; then again, performing a small massacre was no unfit venture in the ugly heart of the horrible and wretched Larry the Lizard. The door was open, and darkness peered out from within.

Larry did not sense anything as he approached. All had seemed of a normality, too, on his journey through town beneath the dark of night in the early hours of morning. All but for a feeling, that is, of being unearthed, removed from powers, worry beseeching him. Weakened by apprehension, he rushed into his dead wife's apartment. Unnerved, he felt he saw, or half saw, a grey hare hop under his feet. He turned before entering the apartment, and near stumbled and fell, but the hare was gone; and further unsure of the elements at play that night Larry wandered through the dark of his wife's flat. It came over him then: the moon had vanished from the sky, as earlier in the evening it had beamed a bright golden, it was gone and naught but a starless black and the dull lights of streetlamps had watched Larry's path through town. Fear dwelt in him ever the more, his apprehension quickening.

In a dark corner of the apartment, found he his wife. Dead, her body closed up, snapped shut at the waist, her back like a hard rock: her carcass like a gigantic oyster concealing her remains. A deep coldness hovered about her corpse and the stone shell upon her back. Larry opened her then, lifting the shell with one claw, and he reached in and felt through the glutinous and gooey mass of his dead wife as a venomous reek seeped into the air. He grimaced, eventually pulling a small, round node of flesh out in one hand, and dropped the weight of the shell so that it closed and gushed one final waft of stench. That was when Larry felt something around him, his antennae-like senses returning from beyond the haze of his apprehension: he was being watched;

his scales turned hard like plates of stone and he stood as tall as he could, before his head came to scrape on the ceiling.

Around he turned and what he saw was as this: three women with long white hair, one facing him, another left and the other right. They saluted with raised swords, silver and gleaming the blades, and in her right hand held the woman facing him a large torch and the apartment was aflame with light and all darkness had been removed. Their faces were fascinatingly beautiful, their figures both voluptuous and slight, and each were they identical, and, at a glance, the women had captured Larry's heart,—yet scorn, a foreboding wrath, seemed to glare from within their eyes and to haunt their expressions; their feet hissing, like they stood upon the backs of many snakes. As they vanished, before Larry could think to act or speak, with a wind that all at once came from nowhere, inhaled into the floorboards beneath, the baying of viscous hounds snapped with unseen jaws at Larry's ankles and feet.

"Drown him," whispered a voice, as though submerged somewhere beneath a body of water. Larry heard four taps in the bathroom turn then at once and water begin to gush. Hearing then the toilet flush and the shower switch on, angered, he rushed across the unlit apartment, into the bathroom where a figure stood waiting; a swarm of shadows, taking on no anthropoid form, but hovering and convulsing; malevolent and unbound. The sink taps, the bath, the shower head and toilet erupted with jets of water.

"Drown him," the shapeless figure spoke into Larry's yellow eyes, and Larry became submerged. He stared into the swarming shadows beneath a room of waters and lunged, slashing, with his claws. The darkness divided, and the water swirled in their wake and vanished, and Larry stood once more, wet and dripping, stone-hard and enormous in the breathable space of the bathroom.

Out of the building he slunk and into the night. Lights flickered on in the distance behind him, the grey building he had left, never again to return, coming alive with the shouting voices of men; and in the night skies heard he three howls rise and Larry looked up to see a dark spot in the heavens, a dark moon emitting dark rays.

Larry crouched in a hidden corner outside the glare of streetlamps, behind four empty dumpsters, and he lifted to his face the pearl that had been his wife's black heart; a white pearl: a pearl of great price.

#

At the apartment of his last victim Larry kept the man whom had slain his wife, while he sat in a red glow of the setting sun. He stared out a window, the drapes partially drawn, upon an old chair, the man he held captive bound and gagged and wrapped in black satin, lying atop the bed, for the journey Larry had to take; Larry waited. Clothed in his grey suit which rarely he removed and never he washed, his red tie loose about his neck. Larry stared out the window, the red setting sun catching in his yellow eyes, and he played with his tail, long, green and scaled, thick at the base, slender and sharp toward the end, curling it through the air, gently, about his head.

Larry was going to take a walk when the sun had set and twilight began to pass.

#

Green scaled hand reaching out the open sewer to pull back in-place the manhole cover, Larry heard as that lid did slide and scrape along the ground, over the loudness of its metallic whisper, an owl screech; and hot eyes burnt his hand. Larry climbed down the sewer with the man wrapped in black satin over one shoulder. He made then his way through winding tunnels, swam through waters that never a man had seen, skipped over rivers and idle little streams.

And then again he saw it, the hare. It was at the end of a narrow, distantly lit tunnel he had almost to crawl to get through. The hare hopped away before him and into the light beyond.

It was a soft and gentle light; glowing mist. Larry climbed out the end of the tunnel and he stood, pulling his cargo through by rope.

The hare was close to Larry and sat beneath a willow tree with long, beautiful vines of sky-blue leaves and a great many reaching and tangled roots that stretched into a dense, black water. The ground beneath Larry's feet was of moss, soft underfoot and a dark green. The hare sat and stared up at Larry from beneath the willow, and then it turned its grey hide and it hoped across the water extending out from the bed of moss, under the blue-leaved willow tree; into an ambient darkness the hare vanished; its feet making not a puddle as it hopped, not a sound.

Larry took seat on the mossy ground, his scaled back pressed against the tree. The man wrapped and bound had fallen asleep and made not a fidget of noise, but heavily breathed. Larry stared into the blackness across the water and beyond the mist, where seemed there only to be darkness. He stared for a while and sometime, until the silence became broken by a horrid noise of wailing and gnashing teeth.

The pearl began to grow hot in his hand, and Larry had to unfurl his claws and remove it from out a crease in his palm. It glowed golden in his green palm, gently brushing his black claws with its light. Larry breathed deeply and looked up at the willow tree and its vines of sky-blue leaves: he swallowed the pearl, and with the man wrapped in black satin under his arm, the rope tied tightly around his right palm, Larry slipped into dark, reflection-less waters and sank far, far beneath.

PART III

Larry floated to the surface of a wide and vast sea. He emerged and as he met the air he awoke and he gasped and he inhaled. He swam toward the shore immediately in his vision, his right arm pulling the weight of the man who'd slew his wife. Larry crawled onto the shore. He pulled the man from the water. The man did not wake, did not move. The man hadn't survived the journey, and Larry hadn't expected him to. For without a pearl, or an accompanying Goddess, not a man, or a lizard, or beast of any kind, could survive the descent, the transition between worlds;—even if one was equipped with gills, one would not properly transmute and would either die or ever find themselves sinking downward, never to rise, never to find birth in the water of the wide and vast sea as Larry had.

He remembered not the shore, for he had been but a babe when first had he emerged. The shore was decorated with the many faces of shells covering a grey sand; shells round and bright and fleshy. Larry had to be careful as he trod over the bright, round shells, for some had hard and sharp tips, whilst yet, those which were soft oozed with a sweet smell as Larry gently trod across the shore (and this distracted him some, causing he to step occasionally on a sharp node), his feet never once touching the grey sands that lay beneath for the many pink and white and silver, golden and bronze shells. He stopped when he was clear of the sand and the shells and a green grass grew underfoot, and he turned to gaze at the sea, place of his brith—primordial womb—his cargo limp over one shoulder.

Clouds formed like a great ceiling in the sky above the sea, the waters were calm and still, but the sky seemed to swirl and the eye of a storm to stare down at the waters beneath, with a black face, singing many curses, and the sea was but black for the sky. Larry felt the sapling creature of his heart long for the touch of mother.

Larry was weakened by the journey far beneath and a great sleep which had seen him there; his scales felt as slime; his breathing was thin and tapered.

Larry headed west. There was no sun in the sky, no moon or stars, the air but held a pleasant glow like as a fine vapour. It was not for a long walk that Larry saw a light in the sky, the light of a moon, and it was purple, and upon meeting with Larry's eyes he felt distant from the body, light, suddenly tireless; next he noticed that his body was not even dense anymore. He had become as a spectre, a ghost, his green scales a perfect mirage in the shimmering purple rays of a translucent moon in the gaining sky.

He walked on through the grassy field and he noticed his cargo had become pale and ghostly, also; weightless. Larry found untold speed in his steps, and he leapt.

In the horizon came into sight another moon, a pink moon, and as its light filled Larry's eyes his head surged with pressure, and density partially returned to his flesh.

The wind which had blown without touching him now blew with a faint, cold air, near unnoticeable bitterness; and Larry heard, as if the crying voice of a woman was upon the air, the wind sigh and heave and moan delicately in a chamber just in-between hearing. A path appeared ahead and Larry stopped before it as he gazed into the pink light of a blue horizon.

It was upon the path ahead that the grey hare reappeared to Larry. It hopped away, turning from him, and made along the path, headed west. The path underfoot was made of bone, and Larry saw then and noticed that the ground had become barren, hard sand reaching as far as his eyes saw, both ahead and behind, left and right. The Path of Bones was a great spinal column set in the yellow sand. Pink and shimmering moonlight became clearer in the sky as Larry walked.

Could not now Larry leap as once before, but still, running delicately upon the ridges of the Path of Bone, he traversed with formidable speed, and the hare, seeming illusive in its own material quality and form, like a small drifting grey haze in the distance ahead, lead the way into the horizon and the beams of the pink moon.

The light of the pink moon vanished behind him, and in front came then no further light, no further moon, just the bright mist of the air and the blue sky above and a forest that slowly came into view. The hare stopped at the edge of a woodland, green and thick with shrubbery, ground laden with tangled roots, dangling vines wiggling from trees, and tall standing grass which hid the ruffle and stir of many a wild creature. Larry halted at the entrance, feeling suddenly his flesh return and grow somewhat denser being absent the pink moon's light. He chose to slink carefully, for what of the creatures that lurked in the jungle he did not know.

Larry entered through foliage, many a catching vine being his first troublesome obstacle, and then narrow gaps between trees—so that he had to climb high the branches of one tree and then climb to the next; and so Larry jumped and leaped and swung from tree to tree, carrying his dead passenger for the Queen. Density had returned mildly to Larry's spectral form, but still he was lighter than he had been in the world above, and for that reason he swung almost soundlessly, like a wind or gentle breeze, through the heavily tangled jungle, making a great and half-terrified effort to remain over the narrow path, the spine that lay in the ground, that he never leave its tracks, that it remained always beneath him; for Larry had gained a terrible feeling the moment he saw it, like a fleeting memory, a feeling that spoke loudly to him and told him not to venture, for any distraction, any perfumed scent, alluring rose, from the narrow Path of Bone.

It was not until Larry spotted a new moon that he saw again the hare. The moon that came into sight, through gaps in the branches of trees and a thick, green and twisted canopy of the forest, was blue. It's light matched with the sky and would have painted the dark corners of the woodland with a peaceful, shimmering light if it was that darkness could exist where the air held like a transparent mist, faintly, perceivable glow; thus all the skies were filled with light, and each moon came only to add dapples of colour to where it might, and not to illumine the darkness.

The hare stopped in a place where the moon shone bright its blue hue upon the narrow path within the forest, and Larry stopped to gaze upon the hare; its head was upturned to him and its whiskers and nose seemed to twitch in his direction. It turned and slowly ventured further through thickets, beyond that Larry could see.

The canopy disappearing as Larry swung through an ample gap in a cloud of branches and leaves from one tree to the next, all sight became flooded with a magnificent moon's blue and shimmering light, and he saw, absent any woodland, a great expanse before him of green grasses, tall and waving in a warm, tranquil wind; large rocks here and there alone, a twinkling grey of fossil and mineral. The Path of Bone lost to the grasses, Larry fell to the earth, alert, suspicious of the wind's soothing warmth.

With the man cocooned in black satin safely atop the ridges of his back, Larry crawled into the grasses, following closely the narrow path, enormous vertebrae from grounds risen. The blue moon stroking his skin with its light, the grasses stroking his sides, the wind blowing beneath him, warming his belly, he ventured through the tall grasses, feeling becoming greater, density returning to his ghost-like form. And then beasts sounded about all the grass. Larry stood tall, and he made his power told, his scales became as hard, impenetrable plates of green rock. Larry was feeling hot, and his blood seemed to have returned to his form, and when he heard several beasts ahead, their roaring and screeching and grunting stirring in the grasses around, Larry hissed and blared a deafening cry into the air, a cry that would on lands above have punctured the ear drums, swollen and made bloody the canals of ordinary listeners. The beast's ahead and around him in their clamour subsided. And so, picking up the man whom had slain his wife, Larry continued on, crawling, his form long-reaching in front and behind.

A distance he pressed and no other beast heard he scream, roar, wail or cry, none; not a sound until a lovely tune, made finer all the more by the presence of a blue and pleasurable moon directly overhead, reached his ears upon soft and warm winds. Larry bid the song that greet him no cry or wail or scream, no aggression; Larry stopped and but listened, and his flesh grew ever more with feeling and the flesh between his legs pulsed with copious blood, and in his spectral form that he still slightly wore, he lusted. Quickly he pressed on, hypnotism in his eyes, and what he saw where the grasses grew low and rocks sat high with glistening grey surfaces of a rainbow of minerals, was a young, beautiful maiden with pale blue eyes, a black head of hair and brown feathered wings; her flesh was bare and her music a seduction to Larry.

With Larry's eyes met she with a soft entrance of her own, a promise of love by touch. She played a golden harp and she played it beautifully, each note drawing Larry further to her; the lower half of her, however, the half that sat upon the glistening rock, Larry then saw was of a bird, and that she had talons, and filthy-brown feathers covering crooked legs. And he looked away, his ears still filled with the music of the harp, to only become he further entranced when a second beautiful maiden drifted down on a current of wind and brown wings; playing a silver flute.

Landing this second naked maiden upon the rock with the first, Larry saw them to be sisters, their characteristics alike. A voice rose into the air and a third maiden came into sight, third of sisters saw Larry, with pale blue eyes and a head of long black hair, descending from high over Larry's head to drift and hover low and close to he as she drew unto herself the moon's light so that she glowed from all corners with it; and her words came upon Larry, never-ending, and Larry lost their beginning as bathed he in the ambiance of blue light and music. Time and place quickly a vacant purpose Larry could not remember, and Larry was lulled to step away from the path in the grasses; but Larry, as the flesh between his scaled legs throbbed and his form grew with a greater lustful density, Larry saw a wickedness upon the maiden's faces, and the spell of music and of song left him for the *dark beauty* of these winged beasts; he shook off the net of hypnotism and scuttled along the narrow path, their screeches and screams assailing the air; and all forms of beast in the tall grasses ahead and behind took to a chorus of horrid cries. The three maidens screeched to the heavens, and when Larry gained distance so that the grasses disappeared, their moans pitched to final, deafening notes, and Larry thought them to have surely died.

The blue moon far behind, Larry grew denser, and when it vanished, ahead the grey hare hopping, from the blue skies of a distant horizon saw he then a green moon come into sight and his eyes filled with joy.

The green light was soft, whispering of secret love, and around him were low golden grasses, and Larry stood tall from the ground. Larry grew denser in the green light, and as the green moon moved overhead in the sky, Larry began to feel surging pains in his chest, and then his heart throbbed and felt he a terrible sadness. By great, wrenching pangs Larry was thrown to his knees beneath the green moon as it arrived in the zenith of the sky. His heart beat as though heavy with blood that would not flow, hard in his chest. He felt his heart stop but he did not die, he *burned*, his body in great and sudden flames.

The hare was at his face when he looked up. Larry smiled with his teeth and the hare jumped away, seeming almost playful. Larry stood up, and the fires were gone; so was the moon, and the low golden grasses; and a barren and cracked earth was underfoot.

In the horizon came the next moon as the hare bounded ahead and Larry caught up close to its tail, a moon that shone like the sun and emitted cool heats. It was yellow and had ten deep blue petals of flame.

Larry ran across a growingly hot earth, upon the vertebrae from grounds beneath, feeling power stir in his flesh, and his eyes glowed a magnificent yellow, deep and projecting into the cool air ahead, and his chest swam with a great abundance of heat, and his will was cool, yet powerful. The moon blazoned and wavered like the Sahara sun the closer it came in the zenith. Its light yet soft, calming. The blue petals of the yellow moon wavered and flickered in the sky, stretched and expanded, contracting, shimmering along the seams, like wiggling tongues of bright blue flame set in a patient light-blue sea.

Overhead when the yellow moon reached and perched in the zenith of the sky Larry looked to the heat of the earth and saw that the ground was as fire, yellow flames; heat rose, gushed up. As he made away from the brilliant brightness of the yellow moon, its petals of blue flame becoming smaller in a distance behind, the earth became cool and the yellow flame retreated beneath its hard surface.

Larry shrunk from an enormous and raging size the brilliance of the yellow moon's light had stimulated his body into erection of.

Larry grew in density when the light of the yellow moon vanished, filled more by his flesh, and appeared then from the horizon ahead of the hare a white moon. Larry felt denser than ever he had upon the land high above that for a number of millennia he had dwelt. He felt heavy, and his flesh was a weight he must carry now.

The moon was a crescent and its light was faintly pleasurable from its distance in the sky of the horizon. But as Larry gained closer, and closer, the white moon gained in size, and from being a slither of white, crescent light it steadily became full and radiated with *nurturing* beams that grew ever more with ecstasy as laden its drug became in Larry's flesh and eyes; his flesh having too become lighter from the white glow of the moon and its intoxicating affect, he felt again ghost-like as had he beneath the purple moon, free to jump and move down the narrow Path of Bone as he wished. So carefree did Larry become in the white brilliance of the moon that not did he realise the hare having vanished from sight, and not did he realise from where the cool and liquid feeling about him had come; not did he realise the flowing stream about his waist, flooding the narrow path and washing across the earth to the horizons. A bright flame flashed in Larry's eyes and, his vision stolen to the right, he saw three women with long white hair and of identical bodies and fascinating facial features, and he saw their swords raised high and a darkness in their eyes; and the torch one held illuminated his face, and their warning was upon him and dogs howled and bayed in an encircling distance of the sky; the moon came into the zenith and no longer was it white then but orange, and no longer was their a cool feeling about him of a waist high stream but dry and barren land and a searing pain in his feet and in the sudden encumbering of flesh.

Larry fell to all fours and he cried. And the orange moon's light suffocated him, unbearably hot, and his veins throbbed, uncontrollably. His vision went black. Purple eyes came then and met him in the darkness of his mind and with a benevolent stare they asked: *Why, why have you become lost?* And they reminded him: *The path is underfoot. Stand, walk.*

In darkness he crawled, and in darkness he found a light. Further he crawled, further the light grew in the dark of his vision, and he saw that the light was the hare and that it was silver and shinning, and he stood, and he walked toward the light of the hare, and his vision returned, and behind him a crescent moon faintly beamed, stroking him with white, soothing rays of nourishing light as away Larry slunk.

Red beams bled into a sky's darkening belly, but Larry felt too weak to continue; yet those eyes, their purple and benevolent glare, remained and gave him strength. Larry, heavily encumbered with flesh and density now, plodded toward the new moon and red light of a darkening blue sky. He retained his cargo, the man wrapped in black satin, retained him by the rope still fastened around one palm. He pulled the man in by the rope and with him underarm, Larry the Lizard increased the pace of his march and followed the grey hare into a red moon's light and a darkening sky.

Under twilight Larry eventually found hisself, the glowing air of the plane seeming to die, darkness giving hail to the forthcoming of a night. As though punctured and bleeding the sky appeared, a wound drawn like a moon in the gathering darkness of deepening blue. The air gradually wailed, at first only whispering of some silent cry, but a wailing was now apparent in Larry's ears, and more so as he reached closer the red moon in the sky. And how far he had travelled. If the encouragement of the benevolent eyes were true, the Queen lie not far ahead. And if untrue, if the Queen lie not close ahead but far, far away, too far to continue, would Larry become consumed by this wailing? He began thinking as such when the wailing became awful loud and the red moon grew both larger and closer, daunting in its form as over him it seemed to yawn and long to swallow him whole; darkness covered the land; and the moon's beams gained heavenward were thwarted before they reached the ground, and they abstained from sharing light with the earth, withholding blood-red rays meters high. Larry passed the gaping, red wound of the darkening blue, and as pass he did, as the wailing grew, the many faucets, many faces, that were the source of the outpouring clamour, the cries, revealed themselves in the darkness beneath red light.

Black puddles, scattered across the barren earth, between them, around them, inside of them, babes that resembled Larry, that resembled the sapling of his heart, wailed malnourished, unclothed in a darkness beneath a sea of blood-red light. And a great loneliness and bitterness filled Larry's heart, and felt he defeated upon this, as though never would he reach the Queen, and his hope abandoned him.

Powerless, weak, the wailing consuming him, black puddles seeming to cry out with his name in the language of his tongue, he thinking of leaping from the path and diving head first into the blackness of one near to his left, as if in doing so he would vanish, but the sapling in his heart cried for mother, for Queen, and he chose to walk for his own integrity and his Queen's honour into a presumed fate of both failure and doom, and as so he did, as so the gaping, thirsty blood moon of the sky sank to a horizon behind, Larry felt lift from hisself the hopelessness of defeat. And he saw as he looked back at that moon, the gaping wound that it was, he saw it converge with the earth, closing its light from his distance where he stood, and as the horizon closed upon the red moon, converging with its thirsty light, darkness darted across the land.

In that most supreme darkness Larry found way by the torches of his yellow eyes. The hare was waiting for him, saw he by luminous, yellow beams of his vision, and he felt strangely sure that he was not far from journey's end. Wide and thick had the Path of Bone underfoot become, as though of the pelvis. Darkness had become truly stark, and a heaviness came with it, and each step Larry took was attached to a sinking weight that stole his legs deeper and deeper into cold sand. A dark moon appeared, and not far ahead but quite sudden, illumination being thus given to darkness; and Larry saw his Queen's abode; saw the dark moon, full and round and emitting a light both luminous and black, and, beneath that dark moon, a city in clouds, a city of tall grey buildings and amber, artificial lights; a whirling of noise fell from the heaven and that platform city in the sky; and the moon beamed with a dark power over the tall, grey buildings, and Larry, far beneath.

Another brightness Larry beheld and gazed upon and became enthralled by a will to traverse the final sands to the Queen's front door; a column reaching into the sky, a column that rose from the Queen's lair, rose high and into blackness, rose with a brilliant white light; a column of ascent.

Larry's feet had sunk into the cold sand so that it became that he could not step from the sand for the density and depth of the sand that had caught him. The hare ahead however, silver and shinning in darkness and illumination, hopped to the front door of the Queen's unmistakable lair: what looked from outside like the face of a stark grey cliff of jagged and ridged rock assailing to a mighty altitude, was that lair; and as the hare hopped to the face of it, there it opened, grey walls sliding away to reveal the recess of a cave. In the magnificent cliff of rock glistening with fossils and minerals of a myriad of colours Larry saw a gentle pink light come glimmering, come escaping; and this light freed him from the sands

and forward into that light he sprung, following the hare through the cave-like entrance, a perfumed scent quickly filling his nostrils and lungs as he entered.

Inside the lair of the Queen there were many faces of other lizards, some were taller than Larry, some smaller, some wider and larger, some slimmer, some green, some yellow, some orange, some blue, and some black; they lined the walls and from afar flanked a white carpet that Larry found under his feet. Beside the carpet of a white silk, on each side, stood and glared the beautiful figures and smiling warm faces, soft lips and bright eyes of seven welcoming maidens: daughters of the Queen. The floor and ceiling and walls were all made of gold and black, glinting volcanic glass, and all was bathed, entranced in a pink, soft glowing of light.

The hare hopped along the white silken carpet and found the Queen, and hopped into the lap of the Queen, and the Queen held the hare in delicate, white hands. The hare sat comfortably and began to sleep in the lap of the Queen, and Larry rushed up the carpet, with his cargo retained underarm, to stand tall and proud and worthy before Her Majesty.

Larry smiled wide, with all of his teeth, bright yellow eyes aswirl, and he stood as tall as he could. "Enough," She said. "My child. Come hither closer that we might speak."

And so Larry, recoiling his height, stood before the Queen, beneath Her throne, and She was as this: purple, enchanting eyes; golden, bright hair, long and reaching past Her waist; skin a delicate white, red cheeks alive with blood; Her lips were a purple kiss as She spoke; and Her flesh was bare but for the covering of a transparent white gown of silk; wings were furled at Her back, white and of brilliant light; and upon Her golden head of hair rested an amethyst crown adorned with seven white pearls; and before Larry She was vision of visions, Her flesh the most warming, pleasing sight to his eyes; and Her breasts, covered with silken gown, were like a treasure Larry ached to reveal as beheld he the Queen Mother, nurturer to his kind.

Her throne was an enormous shell, pink oyster, emitting a tranquil light. Upon the back of Her throne sat there an owl of dark-brown feathers, its eyes closed, its breath unconscious, its talons clutching ever the shell of the Queen. The Queen spoke again, and Larry's eyes were drawn to the purple kiss of Her lips, and She said, "I know that you are innocent of murdering your wife. Please, place the man you have brought with you down." Larry did as the Queen bade him, and She continued, "And, my dear, come to me." She curled an elegant finger toward Herself and She revealed to him Her breasts, and Larry crawled to Her, drawn by the succulent beauty and roundness of Her flesh. How he could only but vaguely remember his wife's two breasts when had they been firm and oozing for him their precious milk. Larry moved to Her, step by step, to the Queen's oyster throne and Her uncovered breasts, thinking suddenly of the staleness that had grown within his wife's bosom, and then he saw Her, the Queen, how Her eyes, ever beautiful, glimmered with fine points of light.

"That's right, my dear, suckle mother's flesh," said She. He saw the light in Her eyes and how it entranced him, but before him, too, he saw the bare flesh of his Queen and all of Her beauty and saw that She was splendid beyond all creatures. And Larry walked up the steps to Her throne, and finally, bent the knee before

Her, and lowered his head, and the Queen, reaching with Her right hand raised Larry's face by Her touch and Larry rose to his feet; and laying his hands on the Queen's naked flesh, he was filled with warmth, and he embraced Her smell, bringing close his scaled face to Her white, brilliant skin, and he fondled and squeezed Her, adoringly. He drank Her precious milk that for so long had he not found the satisfaction of. Her voice filled his ears with a sweet moan and he was taken away on streams of pleasure, and warmth, and joy as the scents of his Queen filled his heart and lust burnt between them like a shinning star.

Larry saw in his mind Her purple, entrancing eyes, and their soft glare, and heard he PIERCINGLY loud Her moaning grow, and with a cackling, the river of pleasure that had swept him became suddenly disturbed; and gone was the Queen from his arms, and gone was he from Her. He felt a searing pain across his limbs, and when next he opened his eyes he was strewn across a golden bowl, and his arms and legs were not of him but apart from him and they sat around him in the bowl, and saw he that the Queen's lizards had decapitated him. As he lay there in a golden bowl the Queen's voice filled him sweetly, like a glimmering sound, but he could not hear Her words.

The Queen stood before him and She spoke briefly, and She turned then, Her purple eyes leaving Larry, Her golden hair growing into a distance away from Larry's eyes; and the daughters of the Queen flocked around him and they introduced themselves as: Ruby, and Topaz, and Sunstone, Emerald, and Sapphire, and two twins both by the name of Amethyst and conjoined were they at the waist.

Each wore a black satin dress; and each of the daughters of the Queen were seductive to lay eyes upon and each held they characteristics by colour of hair, lips and eyes as to their name.

The column of light ascending from out the Queen's lair shone ferociously, far aback Her oyster throne, and Larry's eyes glimpsed the sight of Her Majesty in a stasis as she rose into the air with the column of light, and She was cackling, and glowing. And Her daughters quickly grabbed Larry's limbs, head and torso, and they put him into a black satin sack and carried him away.

EPILOGUE

The following is private documentation regarding a matter of utmost importance to the safety, security and integrity of King and Country. A number of incidents and unsolved cases have been strung together by the Authoritarian Strongholds of major cities belonging to The State. Lastly, whence the suspect is presumed to have thrived, Maya Metropolis, currently under strict quarantine to hold tight the suspect within our sweeping vision, is fully cooperating with the task force enlisted by His Majesty's royal government: a private sector, known as S. N. A. K. E..

All documentation henceforth that you are currently extorting with your eyes should hereby be put down, unless, of course, your eyes are not improper to view the documents at hand. The federal warning *Red* has been stamped upon these documents. Please avert your eyes and return these papers to the authority whom will politely detain and question you, innocent citizen of The State, as to your discovery of these papers.

Maya Metropolis, Authoritarian Summary of Evidence and Crimes (case number, 467038):—

I am writing this summary for the use of government adjourned private sector S. N. A. K. E., and will summarise the precipitous mound of evidence my detectives have linked to the discovery and identity of a serial killer and his whereabouts in the fine and upstanding city of Maya.

The suspect remains at large and the speculation is wide and varying. Across major cities and some smaller towns and villages strange disappearances have been recorded for the last two millennia; *strange descriptions* having been filed away by the Authoritarian Strongholds of The State, such descriptions having now found use in the emergence of an individual whose victim surplus has recently come into discovery;—these descriptions are of interest, despite how bizarre they may seem, my detectives believe, as they have heard the same audacious and troubling remarks, confusion, sure short-sightedness, come from persons they have in the city of Maya interviewed regarding a one 'Larry'.

Littering the bed of the river Sticks was his surplus of victims found, and upon close investigation of CCTV of the nearby area, a person was discovered visiting the river, frequently, carrying what looks to have been a large sack—no identification has been afforded to this person; however, an individual of similar dimensions was seen by further CCTV footage across town carrying what looked to be a body wrapped in fabric—the two are being linked; the same individual was caught on CCTV entering the sewers—Maya's sewer system is currently now under the close inspection of S. N. A. K. E..

Following investigation by my detectives a man's name emerged. An unusual creature was also discovered, dead, at the top of a building of apartments (note: all documentation is being transferred, as requested). The man we are suspecting goes by the name of Larry (and, the name my team has assigned to him: 'Larry the Lizard'); no other names have been afforded to the suspect.

Also, with the documentation at present, we are disclosing a physical piece of evidence along with recent lab analysis reports. A mask was found outside the suspect's place of work the same day he stopped showing up. The mask is unusual and alarming, being it firstly a mask of no more than a wide and smiling pair of lips, the lower half of someone's face. Reports have told us that it is both real and human. The mask is strangely preserved, its age dating back over a millennia. The man whom found the mask is no other than the car showroom manager at the suspect's place of work. He has filed a statement upon handing the evidence in. It were his words that the mask filled him with 'an eerie feeling', and that in his statement he professed to the smile belonging to no other than our suspect and his missing employee, Larry. It is unusual and cryptically sinister, indeed. It is more troubling when the lab analysis is taken into full consideration; for a reported green slime having being found on the inside of the human mask has been recognised as belonging to that of the lizard's genome; such evidence placed into this unutterable case fills myself, and my detectives, with inconsolable chills.

Following here in this documentation are the written recordings of interviews held with various persons willing to come forward with information on Larry, A. K. A., Larry the Lizard. We hope that the evidence acquired will be of service to S. N. A. K. E. in the apprehension of the killer, or killers, that still to this day, with Maya Metropolis under quarantine, and full cooperation of the Authoritarian Stronghold pledged to S. N. A. K. E. (at His Majesty's request), remain at large.

Long live the King.

Commanding Chief and Officer,
Nigel G. Winttahouws

The following recordings are official and private documentation of the Maya Metropolis Authoritarian Stronghold. The interviewer's names are being withheld from these papers, as are the names of the interviewees (such information is already in the hands of S. N. A. K. E. and it is their wish that personal information not be afforded to separate and varying documentation).

—Interview One—

The person interviewed is an elderly lady of seventy-two years, and she lived near the suspect's place of work, seeing him pass by her home regularly.

Interviewer: "Could you please describe to us your relationship with Larry?"

Interviewee: "Well, we didn't really have a relationship, but of course I can tell you what I knew of him." She paused and looked to her feet. After fidgeting in her chair, she continued, "Well, I never knew him by name. He would pass me on a morning sometimes. I wake early, and sometimes I go out into my back garden or I look from my front windows. I would recognise him as a man that works at the car showroom up the road from me. I always suspected he was just walking to work, rather early. It was usually before the sun had risen that I'd see him, you see.

"Though I stopped looking out of my front window following what I believed I saw one day as he had walked by. I went to my doctor about it and he tried to blame it on a migraine I'd been experiencing the day before. Anyway, so there I was, enjoying the first moments of light over the day and then there he was, and I swore he glanced up at me, but I don't know because my eyes stung terribly, and when he passed by and my vision stopped hurting, I looked again, and I thought I saw a tail!"

Interviewer: "Did you say a *tail*?"

Interviewee: "Yes! And it was long and green. Honestly, I don't know what I saw. Part of me believes it, part of me doesn't want to. Part of me feels as though I saw a horrible truth that morning, and ever since, I stopped looking out my front windows. I haven't seen him since then."

Interviewer: "And is that as far as your relationship with the man in question extends?"

Interviewee: "Yes... well, no. There's one more thing. A rabbit."

Interviewer: "A rabbit?"

Interviewee: "Yes. I used to rather enjoy watching him walk by on mornings, because I half fancied that he kept a pet rabbit that sometimes I would see following him, or in front of him. He never seemed to be aware of it, but I imagined it was his and he let it out on a morning; after that I didn't know where it went, nor have I ever seen it since I stopped looking from my front windows—since he glared up at me and I saw his tail."

Interviewer: "Thank you, ma'am, you've been a great help."

Interviewee: "So, this... Larry is missing now? Should I be worried?"

Interviewer: "Yes ma'am, but there's no reason we should suspect he would target you."

Interviewee: "What is it he's done exactly—have others seen his tail?"

Interviewer: "We aren't at liberty to disclose such facts, ma'am."

Interviewee: "Does this mean I can start looking out my front windows again? If he's missing then, I mean?"

Interviewer: "If it doesn't affect your health, ma'am, I would say it's safe. Thank you for your time."

—Interview Two—

The interviewee was a female colleague of Larry's, of 23 years of age, whom still works at the car showroom that Larry is believed to have been in employment of.

Interviewer: "Could you tell us your role at the showroom?"

Interviewee: "I'm the receptionist."

Interviewer: "Okay. And your relationship with Larry?"

Interviewee: "Oh, is that who you wanted to question me about. Well. Me and Larry have a little bit of history, but nothing too juicy. He didn't really talk to anyone, but everyone liked him, and he was always smiling. He smelled nice too."

Interviewer: "And your relationship, miss?"

Interviewee: "Oh, yes, that. Well. Me and Larry were sort of friends. More than any of the others at least. I always fancied that he liked me. And then one day, whilst I was feeling all infatuated with his smell—he smells so nice—he came out of his office, and it was all dark in there, and he asked me to follow him, and I did, and, well... I tell you. He is a big guy but I've never been so soar in my life."

Interviewer: "So you had sex with him?"

Interviewee: "I did."

Interviewer: "Was there anything unusual that you noticed?"

Interviewee: "Well. Apart from how big he was. Not really. Uhm. He threw me on his desk and tore my clothes off. I was surprised. Luckily he had a change of women's clothes in one of his draws. When I asked why he had those there, he smiled and said he had been wanting to do that to me all week. Me and Larry didn't speak much after that, we didn't speak much before it. He was always a quiet guy was Larry. He had beautiful yellow eyes. If you see him can you tell him I've been thinking about him? He doesn't return my calls."

—Interview Three—

The interviewee is male, 45 in years, and was the manager of the car showroom.

Interviewer: "Can you tell us, as the manager of the showroom, how was your relationship with Larry?"

Interviewee: "He was my best salesman. He was always early. I liked him. He gained trust in me."

Interviewer: "Gained trust in you?"

Interviewee: "Yes. He would often stay behind late to do extra work and he would arrive early in the mornings, too. I gave him a spare set of keys to the showroom. I trusted him. And, and he had asked me for them."

Interviewer: "Asked you?"

Interviewee: "Yes. He asked me one morning if he could have a pair. I didn't even think about it, something about him, something in his eyes, he was trustworthy... mhm. Convincing."

Interviewer: "And were there any other dynamics to your relationship? Anything at all strange?"

Interviewee: "Larry was very much a friend. Though we had no communication outside of work. I believe he liked his privacy and solitude. But I allowed him to work as he pleased. On a morning, for instance, I knew he slept in his office for a few hours, but I allowed it because he was my best salesman, and I liked him."

Interviewer: "Did he ever scare you?"

Interviewee: "What do you mean?"

Interviewer: "Scare you, you know, make you uncomfortable."

Interviewee: "Well. I can't believe I'm about to tell you this. I've never told anyone. It was like it didn't actually happen, because afterwards Larry only ever smiled at me, as always he had, always he did.... There was one time that Larry was in my office, and well, I can't remember what we were talking about, I just remember the absurd thought that... that I felt attracted to him. Larry had a fragrance that smelt both like lavender flowers and... and a sun set—"

Interviewer: "—A sun set?"

Interviewee: "Yes. I don't know how else to explain it. But that's how he smelt, or made you feel if he got too close. I was aware of this, and for that reason I avoided staring into his eyes and enjoying his scent too well. Heck, he had his tricks and I didn't want to know them, he sold a lot of cars. Well. This incident I speak of—"

Interviewer: "Did you have an intimate relationship with Larry?"

Interviewee: "No no! Not at all. But well. It was a dream, that's what I've told myself. It never happened. But he was in my office one time, his scent all around me and when I turned around he had closed the door, locked it. My blinds were shut. And his eyes were starring at me. Well. I remember him, inside me." The interviewee pauses. "Or at least I dreamt it. Because when it was over he was gone, and he was talking with a client in his office, and my blinds weren't shut and my door was open."

The following recordings are voicemails taken from Larry's mobile phone found in his office drawers, received from a mother of three whose whole family have gone missing.

Voicemail one: "Larry... are you there?... I want you Larry... I want more of what you gave me in your office... all I've thought about is those eyes, how they gazed into me, how you touched me, so briefly. But I'm married. I have children. And you were so good with them, and me."

Voicemail Two: "It's me again, Larry. I'm going to leave them at home, like you asked, tell them to be good and to sit and wait for mummy. Oh, daddy. It's late and I haven't slept. I don't think I'm going to."

Voicemail Three: "I'm coming now. The sun's up. I'm coming like you asked, Larry. I hope you enjoy your breakfast."

TO BE CONTINUED...

I, THE HIDEOSITY

Darkness surrounds me with yellow eyes as I wait trapped, caged behind bars on a strange new world I know nothing of and have not yet seen the surface up-close, or the skies from down below—only the glancing of perilous seconds, when the engines of my ship exploded, fills my mind and memory, I plunging through a cloud strewn sky. The seas, if seas they have, I have not seen. Vegetation, I have not seen; not have I seen the artefacts observable of any a sustainable plane.—Of the life forms here that inhabit, I, too, know nothing. Albeit, it is life that I came looking for; civilisation, a new society that might accept me for what I am. But all I have seemingly found, so far and to as much as I can deduce, is hostility among a primitive lack of communication.

I don't remember how they took me. All I know is I crashed. All I know is I'm locked in a bare and cold holding cell on an alien plane, that those eyes in the darkness, ten feet above, towering, yellow, monstrous, are watching me, and closely. It might be they are etched with wonder and awe, but they are hostile.

To them, I'm the little green man who came falling out the sky. I'm the fright, which came down in a ball of fire. I am: The Terror;—I, The Alien.

A dehydrated chuckle fills my throat. I laugh. The eyes watch harder, yellower. I am the terror and I am laughing. They back away, fear like sharp and glinting rocks within their eyes, for they are without understanding!, and I laugh harder, harder, my body convulsing to the irony. Oh, how amusing. I, the alien; I, forever alienated; first, by my own society, by my own people; I, ever trapped within the walls of my skin, bound to a like of bone and flesh of grotesque countenance that never did I ask for. And now, a true alien—not a mutant-thing, not anymore.—Before the mercy of these native creatures that I find myself prisoner, it is that I am filled by one question: Will they accept me?

I doubt as much, for fear isn't a friend; therein truly lies the monster, first cause of misunderstanding and realms of violence.

Will they accept me? I can but hope.

This is not completely unlike the reason I left my world, in the first place—for I was alway the 'Little Green Man' back home, alway the alien to whomsoever's eyes I chanced to greet…. Back on my homeplanet, I was a mere, rotten accomplishment borne off the once esteemed man of a notoriously high-prestige; an outcast fledgling of no belonging, I, only I ever belonging to his failure, the darkness where I was kept.

I was my father's first and final mistake, his undoing.

I suppose I haven't anything better to do than whittle to myself. Those eyes, I've already told them the tale, and they just stared. Now it is time I tell you, my Listener, my mind, or God, whosoever listens, wheresoever my Listener may dwell, and whatsoever form you may take: please, I pray to you, have understanding.—Perhaps, perhaps speak?

This, my Dear Listener, is my story (thus far told):

It begins one year ago, today, …he came to me, …my father; came and told me what was expected. The greatness I must account for, project, 'godliness,'—as I so saw it spake in his lips. A great height of expectation awaited, and in the light of him, as he were known, I did feel but a shadow quaking to exist.—No. I was a speck within the shadow cast beneath him, a quaking and unfortunate being within that singular speck. (To the world, I did not yet exist.)

As unsightly as I am to the eye or the ear, people were disturbingly shocked at the aspect of my countenance, ungodly frame, even when I explained to them, the condition of my existence, the truth to my identity, no matter how smoothly explained, it seemed; no, it is always and forever with growing horror that people should discover that which I am; for I am more than human to them, and less; I am more grotesque than the darkest crimes of humanity, and I am far more capable….

My father created me from his own genetic formula, his 'prized' genes one might call them. And he did this in secrecy, for playing God was punishable by death in the modern society which from my father hails. (Barbaric, truly, and counterfeit: for to put to death is to play God.) I believe him, my father, to have already met his fate, for his 'crime'.

He was old, my father. Fading away. I guess he didn't care for the consequences anymore. His like had never been matched, and by his reign within the scientific and the political worlds, he had achieved so much for so, so unspeakably long. I guess he fancied hisself invulnerable, a man above the law, so old and close enough to death not to care (—close enough to death, I say lightly. One could not guess at when my father would actually die, you see, for he had extended his life far beyond the average human's, and was over the age of one-hundred-and-fifty years when I last saw him, and no more aged than a sixty-year-old man of good health). I guess that was the problem. He, not caring. If he had cared, he wouldn't have locked me up and kept me hidden, his son, for near-on twenty years. I guess he never saw it coming; their hate: my forced hand.

All his achievement led him to this. This point of failure. My creation. YES, I am a genius, an intellectual prodigy, I am his greatest achievement,—truly. But I am not like him. I've looked at him for hours whilst he slept. Stared at the symmetry of his face, and then of my own. All his achievements and he can't even get my appearance right. I'm nothing like him! I'm fit only for the waste bin. One look at me and they all shivered, screamed, berated I, The Hideosity.

O', I stand around average height, my limbs are all correct, my movements quite fine. But my appearance, my face, my frame, even this voice, all tainted by the sin which I am devised. My skin hugs to my bones, like sludge. It drapes in places, I tell you. I haven't any lips. My teeth are set so far apart that I whistle when I speak. And my voice, the quality of my voice. Well, compared to the average human, my voice is just a smudge deeper, but it's the way it resonated, each word, how the air crumples when I talk for too long and without pause. Their stomachs churned when I didn't speak slow and spaced for them, the audience. Arhh, the way words slither from my mouth, whistling through the gaps of my teeth, spurting out four ugly holes my father had to puncture for I hadn't an opening to even speak, and have not lips with which I have read are to kiss;—the mere sight of me, the first whisper of a sound I entailed, was enough that they began to cry: *Liar! Liar!* and call for my father's life.—He had betrayed them, only then saw they that he came from the dark.—Funny expression, really, as it is I who lived in darkness, he, why, he strut in the light…. Darkling, they have surely killed him now.

A stage was set for the world to see. Announcing he the unveiling of a new one-man aircraft, one that I designed for him, I, the hideosity. Inter-dimensional travel I told him I had enabled the craft to perform. He revealed this contraption before he chose to expose my alienated self. A 'portal' he called it, a ship designed to explore the unexplored, the unimagined vistas of existence, planes that man had not yet dare consider he reach. He dressed me up smart and expected me to demonstrate to the world my inherited genius, and the capabilities of cloning. (What a mockery.)

Since I began my utilization of will and to read, study, build, invent, devise, his crop field in the scientific industry of inquiry into the Further, the metaphysical, grew rapidly, exponentially, and cast such great shadows across all neighboring efforts and schools of thought that he, he overnight became their ruler. A philosophical idol, they proclaimed him. And he had wanted to expose me sooner, reveal documentation he had kept of my upbringing and creation, but he was afraid to hand over the cream of his success to I—his devisee.

Does godliness have mercy? I ask.

...Forgive me, for I built the ship with hidden intent.

I did not tell him, he did not know. interdimensional travel was not my only intention. My first agenda was to bring my father into a realm of my own devising where he and I would be free; a hemisphere in the heavens where persons are not persecuted, and no evil pervades. That's right, the ship was an escape pod into the farthest ethers, but something happened, something terrible;—something has intervened.

Fear tore through my heart when the people rose up against me, our death apparent in their eyes, upon their tongues; alas!, my second intention came into play, and the ship I have created obliterated them all, the whole crowd; with a one, magnificent heat-ray.

The scorn in my father's eyes when he looked upon me in the aftermath. He stayed; I fled.

#

The eyes. How yellow they glow. How... something is changing, I hear movement behind the dark and the walls. It's time.

They're opening, the bars of my cell, now. I wish I could see! but they've got me in such dark!—whoever you are over there, *have mercy*.

"Hello. You have quite pretty eyes. So golden," I hear myself say to them now they have come more than close enough to listen, hear, perceive, again. "Wait. Careful now. Don't. Ahh. Your hands. Molten glass—of what are you formed?! You're hurting my skin. Please. Where are we going. Please—

"Oh my. What is this? what are you? I don't understand. Say something say something. Speak to me."

A deep voice bleeds overhead, it reverberates within my mind; arhh, how it resounds behind the darkness of my scrunched eyes.

"The Eye calls," I hear, "the Eye calls the Eye calls the Eye calls THE EYE CALLS," until—

bright red lights are jousting through my closed lids,

and the darkness is shattered in which I hide, and I tremble, and am weightless.

My eyes, I open them, and yet it is as though my lids have melted by the power of a strange and enticing red light, and all is but a blurry haze of red that I see. Sights before me beginning to stabilise, scenery comes clear, and... why, what I see is of no less a startling horror than all trials so far I have faced, and the sorrow that has filled this gut. Great chasms with stark rocky faces jeer upward at me. I stand aloft many a gaping and terrifying pits of a haunting bleakness upon the skinny ridge of a sharp cliff's edge, bathed in a red and terrible, yet seducing light, my mind swaying, sense and feeling ultimately ablaze. I cannot breathe.—*O' Lord, where am I?*

A great stench rises on upward winds out the fathomless many granite gullies in the earth. The sky stares down without light, perpetually dark, a swirling mass of volcanic ash and cloud. All is dark, ever dark but for the red light that pierced my closed eyes, coming whence blood-red ores extend with innumerable veins across the grey granite rock of the landscape.

Listener to my mind, bade me answer. Where, O' where am I? Answer me!

I see deep into the chasms between the cliffs from my perch atop a perilously high ridge, into each dry gully, I see dancing, in a great and confused cacophony, a sea of *things*, of creatures; things with arms and legs that move and kick and throw fists, and with their heads they duck and bob; and they weave, like needles through fabric, as they war with one another; and I see, too clearly to describe without flinching, the barbaric assault of women heavy with breast and glutinous curves, long, sharp finger nails like daggers of bone extending from tip of finger, and I see these great feline creatures flail their arms in wicked circles, and I see—

eyeless victims

they wobble, crawl, some lie on their backs unconscious, some prostrate, silently shrieking into the bloodied granite earth; I see creatures whom wield jagged blades that have no craftsmanship and make proud gleam tyrannously of the colour red, the colour of blood, the colour in the damn ores—as they cut and slice through flesh this way and that, maiming without thought, pouring forth more the colour red;

I see things with heads like a snake's, scales enlisted upon cheek and forehead, with snapping jaws and great, unclean, yellow fangs; they move and lumber like tall, creeping shadows, and with their jaws they tear and chew and feed on the flesh of the wounded and the dead; they are a true sorcery of beast, with great necks that bear no flesh, things like serpents grown out the backs of men, great spines reaching into the air, bending over the destruction beneath to rummage the dead and the weak and savage the flesh that lay in many an ungodly heap;

heaves of bodies lie trampled and ruined in the gullies, fed upon, diseased, reeking such foul a stench on the rising gusts of wind; men alive are either intangibly maimed or immutably enraged with a tireless thirst for blood and ruin; I look away then when I see the uncountable instances of rape—I—I, how men, like beasts, their skins black through the smog of darkness that this land lies under, their eyes bright lit by the glow of the ore, and they pierce flesh, flesh dead, flesh alive, grasped in their palms, in their filthy, dirty, savage grasps, pierce with the lusting of the phallus, and there is no separation from the heaps of the dying, the fed upon, the warring, and the lustful.

I must enforce that the use of the word 'men' be interchanged with 'creatures' for dare not I call them human, those which I see, truly and merely retaining they the image of men by form of torso, limbs and head,—anthropoids; and gender, it seems, mirrors humankind, as does plentifully the animal kingdoms; apparent by the singular and long drawn glance I have encountered and mistakenly endured; some hard of form and great in stature, some weak, frail, some skinny and tall, ungainly things that lurch and weave with a quick, untold power, some round, some with curves, and some with the lusty weight of heavy breasts at their chest—all and each of them black as ash or grey as death.

There is no apparent side to them, no union between the forces that far beneath me in the granite gullies fight, no whiff of bravery or defiance do I gain from the upward rising stench that roars upon the wind's foul cry. Such things have I seen.

Never did I dream of this, never, when equations I devised and realms I imagined. Another world, yes. But not this, this is

pure chaos, perfect strife; I have failed to create the realm I desired.

...In which body of the universe do I dwell, I ask. I ask! Nebulous of screaming folly? Pit of my own undoing? Where is the hellfire? Bring me fire and brimstone and do away with these bones, I command thee, O' Listener! I command thee.

Dragged from a mouth in the side of a rocky dune, I was naught but dazed as the red lights of this plane infected my sense of sight. And my ears, for a tundra of cries colliding in the wailing upward wind, filled they with a sickness, like the swaying of a sea existed inside my head; and I bear my eyes now, after the putrid sights of warring things far beneath, only to the ground; and it is that the sickness has fallen to my throat. Curse my eyesight and its genetically enhanced scope.

My arms are numb from the grasp of inhuman hands that hold them, hands sharp and black and hard as obsidian glass. My feet sting and burn as they trail cold, grey granite earth. The beings that bear me, they are not of man, clearly, they are not. Anthropoid, yes. But not are they creatures of a biological inheritance, even. They are but rock born to serve this land, mounds of living, volcanic glass, and as I now lift my head to look up, once again; I see, they are born to serve a great and writhing spiral erect from this plane; a contorting tower.

The Eye calls, the voice that bled over me and into my mind reminds from a distant pocket of memory. The tower I now see looms in the distance to the west against the setting of a deep red sun under the clear sky of a far slung horizon. A great tower is leagues ahead of me, climbing the height of the sky, a spiral of craftsmanship that begs pure madness. It's scale seems faintly to shift and grow and contract as I watch, like a mirage, truly. Its head is a great mushroom cap that thrusts into the black clouds, blacker than the smogs that drift low over the gullies and the swirling ashes of the sky. All darkness is attracted to this one point, to the helm of the tower, like it is a vacuum unto light itself, beacon of ever darkening darknesses, throbbing it and pulsing as though the tower were alive. I shiver as the imagination comes to me of veins wrapped around and encrusting the living walls within the great tower where the sun now sets, red and alive with that terrible, infectious glow of the ores, and a faint heat touches my eyes. O', how they burn!, the glow of red, how it seeps downward through my body. It is heavy and like fire. I cannot. I cannot stay awake.

#

My forehead throbbed and I felt myself falling seamlessly into a dream. It seems now that I am to dream of having fallen asleep however, as suddenly I gaze down, watching from ahigh my little, drooping self carried across the rocky, grey clifftops by men made of glass. Be this all a dream, O' Listener—let this be all a dream.

I, the invisible specter, drift lower to see closer. The beings that carry me glint with beams of red observed from the ground beneath, the ores and veins underfoot, their hard, ridged bodies constructed of black and reflective obsidian glass; they are a shinning haze of darkness and the infectious red. I see myself passed out and limp in their grasps. Blood spills from my arms where they grip me, my flesh thereabout black and seared by the subtle heat of their palms. Their yellow eyes stare forward, bleak, bright and unseeing. They march to the tower. I am a specter and they cannot see me. O' Listener. Have you freed me? Am I dead?

I will myself not to follow. And I am still. I hover high over the ground, over the barren, rocky wasteland of dark smogs and red lights and warring cries riding the backs of the rising winds. All would seem black and dark if not for it were the red light that runs through the granite earth, the red ores with many veins, like a mineral of flesh unto itself. My body beneath is carried further and further away. I wish to leave, I will. I do not want to witness this place. Lord have mercy! I fly high. I will penetrate the clouds. I will—no. No. The red. The swirling mass of clouds and ash are parting, and they give way to a tide of tumbling lights. Red beams cascade down out the sky and engross me, and I am dragged in their wake, downward, downward, plummeting quickly the many leagues I climbed. A screeching sound has filled my vision, and the colour red is all my mind can inhale…. And again, I find myself following those subservient beings of volcanic glass, creatures with yellow eyes I once thought of me frightened!, as they march my body from dark cell of rocky dune to the tower in the far, far distance of a black horizon.

Their legs are as the trunks of trees. What trickery is this I now see? They are walking over the gullies, through the deep chasms that lie between cliffs, high in the air with my body as it swings, their legs extending far, far down to the ground. They crush with their feet dark smogs that drift within the gullies' mouths... they splatter and knock aside the warring fiends that slay and fuck one another as they squirm and hop and dive and flee now in the wake of great slabs of obsidian feet. What trickery is this beyond the scenes already witnessed. These beings are metamorphic? O' Lord, forsake me not. Forsake me not to a realm of such powers! My *mother*. Why am I suddenly now thinking about my mother? I have no mother. I was created as an experiment, I tell you. I see through the parting of dark smogs beneath as beasts like men sunder the soft insides of women, and of other men, too, with the erect flesh between their legs. And I think of having a mother. Where from does this thought come? What is there to learn in the sight of all this madness, should I not tear out my eyes? Arh! My eyes, I have none. I am but mind, or spirit, in this very moment until, I suspect, I slip back into my body and consciousness is regained by the flesh and its sense. What then, I wonder, what then. I stare into the skies, the swirling of ash and clouds is almost peaceful to watch. I will surely awaken in my cell of flesh when into the tower they drag it.

#

Lost I became in a gaze heavenward above the clouds, peace like an immovable star ever burning and ever, very far. How I yearned to be but ash and cloud, black and formless, shifting sleet in high winds. I did not realise how close we had come to the tower, not until through its doors did we reach. Great slabs of stone fell closed, black, impenetrable doors, with the symbol of an eyelid engraved, shut—asleep. And then I awoke in my flesh, inside the tower, to see behind me, with a creaking, snapping noise, the greatness of the two closing doors.

I ascend a flight of winding stairs, O' Listener. I ascend by the pull and drag of beings made of glass, black and glinting with the swirl of lights of various colour that from a pit far beneath, a cellar or dungeon, or some deep hole in the earth!, has come to sting and burn my sense of sight. I hear no noise but the loud screech of and deep ring of what I can only name to be the doom chime of my own despairing heart. I am done. Whatever fate there is atop this winding case of stairs, whatever you wish to happen to I, *O' Listener*, I do not care.

The pain and sting in my eyes retreats into my head and then vanishes. The colour red bleeds through me again as I receive it, reflected from the hard and glinting figures at both my sides as it emits from the walls that are suddenly shimmering about me now as they seem to grow and to contract, alive, to twist and to shift, to crawl and breathe. I can feel not my arms as I am dragged, or my feet which I have glanced and seen tattered and bleeding, bone revealed. A numbness creeps up my legs. My eyes are drawn to the red veins encrusting the encircling tower's inner walls, like we ascend some living monument of dark and panting, stony flesh. Each step upward is made of smooth volcanic glass, obsidian, as, I believe, are the shinning, glinting walls, and the monuments, of course, by which I am carried, dragged. Damn the infernal makeup of this land. Barren rocks and volcanic glass!, black skies and sleet and ash!, damn the maker of this world, this wretched plane.—But not you, O' Listener, not you, of course.

Fine details are ensnaring further my eyes, and I see now fleshy, purple bumps with bright-pink, nobly tips, residing on the glass stairs. Their appearance is so alluring. I cannot help but analyse and stare. I see that they are soft underfoot as I watch glass feet step on them hard and heavy. They ooze a white liquid, thick and creamy, like milk, and a nourishing scent, as though of lavender flowers, with an emerging and gentle spring-heat, rises up to my nostrils, and I am bade a peace, a kind fondling of my heart, an easing to the pains of my aching mind and body. I stop looking around and I am relaxed, all tension having been withdrawn from me. I stare but only down.

Deep and far away, in some pit beneath the tower, I see and calmly gaze into the swirling light—the light that at first as I had entered the darkness of the tower stung terribly my eyes. Vision now glazed with, infected by the red glow from the ores upon walls, I can peer without injury into the light that I describe to you now, O' Listener, as fire. A swirling sea of fires far beneath my ascent, O', and such colours. I see red, and yellow, orange and green, blue and pink. The outer rim burns red, quite like the colour in the veins that line the shifting walls of this mad tower and coarse through every surface of this sick plane you have so damned me to reside! The central fire is pink, and it seems almost to gaze at me, following my eyes. Its light upon my face, I feel myself becoming bathed in pink, warm light, as my body is carried higher and higher. And each step upward fills me with a further, nourishing delight, further ease, comfort, a fondling of my heart as that milk-like substance oozes from the fleshy nodules underfoot and rises like a lavender kiss, warm and soft within these lungs.

Calmness stirs in me like tranquil waters bearing the many faces of a hypnotised reflection; I but feel as though a lake of vapour, breathing mists, untouchable by winds and rain, by the watching of any an eye, within these walls as I ascend. All is dark now. All is peace. Again, I am gone within my mind. Though, no visions entreat me. No. No visions. But… but wait. *Aghh.*— *Father?*

They have hung him by a noose, I see.—I see his body dangling from a rope. He hangs from a monument once erected in his name. A plaque of wood is loose and flaps in a wind about his neck. '*Daemon Bringer*' they branded him by, 'daemon bringer'… his shame.

No, father. What have they done to you?

He is unclothed. His body scathed and marred, bruises and deep, oozing wounds, peels of flesh pulled away to reveal his bones. *Father!* The evil wretches. They are the cursed, not I, not he!

Is this what you wanted, Listener? All of this, this was your plan?

His face is pale and his eyes are sad, desperate, as though through portals from the Underworld I feel he sees, I feel he stares at me; and I feel him reaching through the coldness of grey-blue iris lakes. O' Father. If I only hadn't... obliterated them?, left you behind.

I fall back into my body. A dizzying realisation that the things carrying me have come to a stop descends upon the mind. They are perfectly unmoving, and my heart is greatly slowed, all feeling is numb, as though I am by pains of my heart frozen, intoxicated, drugged, bewitched.

My vision is blurred for the colour red when I look up, and what I see is naught but blotches of smog in a darkness. We are at the head of the tower, that much is clear to me, for the surroundings bathe in a fierce glow of red that does not neglect to illumine my peripheral vision to the dome-like walls and a roof above, and how it is they seem to pulse and to throb, and brighter grows the light, the red. The walls pulse brighter and brighter, the throbbing becomes mad. I shrink within my flesh. O' Listener, reveal thyself to me! Reveal.... A dark mass before us becomes illuminated from out the smog, the dark shroud... a light at once emits from my own eyes as much as it is from the thing opening in darkness. It is oval and hangs between two tall, golden, ridged, unfashioned pillars, jagged and yet with an intangibly smooth sheen to lay upon eyes. How clearly I can see: a purple oval of flesh glowing triumphantly, and my vision is drawn unto it by streams of a gained yellow light, and I know what I am seeing;

I see the Eye, and it wakes.

A great, purple, fleshy eyelid slides up, and I gaze into a dazzling white eye that with grand stream of lights breathes my vision like a ghost out of myself, drawing me unto its mass. Frames of red light are at once blasted and torn from the peripherals of my sight. I am dropped to the floor by hands that release me. My knees scream in terrible agony as they hit an icy coldness underneath—though yet numb feels most of my body. My spine aches at the base. I feel something slither upward my spine. The Eye is so bright and glaring. All is but lost in the blazing whiteness of the Eye as my gaze is drawn to the singular point of its existence, central and staring back, as I travel the stream of light beaming out mine own eyes unto it; I begin to feel a wind, above, feeling being itself by strands still attached to my distancing body, creeping gently through the numbness, and I feel, sense the skies revealed.

The two figures at my sides are pulled from the room by upward currents that rise through the tower. I can hear a swirling, sharp, dangerous hum, like sleet and ash in the spiralling mass of the sky, above, close, and wet, and somehow, somehow nothing is frightening but simply prescribes me with a warmth, and I am comforted. A moisture falls down and wraps around me, like thick, hot rain. I feel cocooned in a delicate womb of heat.

More so and more a gentle heat surging my flesh, inwardly, and the dazzling white light projected of the Eye erupts before me in a spiral of red, yellow, orange, green, blue and pink entrancing fires, and upward, upward I feel slither a serpent alive in my spine; the colours vanish, and in the dazzling white beams of the Eye before me I see someone, O' Listener. What do you show me?—Who is it I see?

The white is subduing and I see in a dark room, beneath the dimness of a single yellow light, a man's face. He looks worried. His features are blurred as he squints. He is tiny, the man that I see. Much smaller than any person I have ever seen or read of, he is... my father. He becomes clearer now. And, agh!, he is hideous, as hideous as I. His limbs are bulgy, his face and neck are swathed with lumps, and his eyes, how tiny are they, how acute his vision must be.

I feel a deep pity for my father, a pity I have cordoned only to myself. Aghast am I, truly. Is this the truth to his form?... How the unseen takes such shape. What ridicule belongs to a world that would never see of such a great man this true and pitiful light, figure, shade of a thing that defies the divinity and essence of his life's works, his luminosity.

He turns now before my vision to light and dust. His frame flashes before me like bright electricity, a skeleton coruscates and then fades into the dark. And he is gone, ever-gone. A breeze whirls about my vision, lazily, and the brightness of dust left behind engulfs me, and again the white and dazzling Eye appears. It is dim this time and I can see its completeness. It closes, blinking once, and reopens, the fleshy purple of the lid drifting and swaying, shaking in the darkness, all engulfed by a tundra of ash and sleet; its purple, fleshy colour spills over the lines that contain it, and the winds take it away.

    —*O' Listener, great Eye, I beg your pardon.*

#

    Bolts of lightening! I am awake. Gone the wicked darkness of that horrible place; the red, infectious ores, and those obsidian walls; the destruction, the chaos in the sky; and the Eye…. I'm—I'm home. The gentle and kind darkness of my room, my four walls, have replaced that resplendent gaze, the divine light of the great Eye I beheld.

    I will not displease you, Listener. *O', Father! Father!* We cannot stay here. I must take him away. My ship. It is intact, surely still. I must secure the laboratory, the hanger. "Father! Come quick, father!"—*Is he even alive?*

    "Why, my son, you're awake?" says a voice walking toward I out of the darkness.

    "We must leave, at once—no time like the present. The people, tomorrow. In the morning. They will hang you for 'playing God'."

    "Son… my son…" I turn to face him, unsure of where he is in the encompassing dark of our home, and he is behind I, or seems to be as I continually turn.

    "I do not know how I will convince you, father. Do not think these words a ploy. But I have been sent here, father, sent back, and to save you. I saw a fate that wasn't right, father. We must use the ship, we must go to another place, now—"

"Son. Please." There are sobs in his voice. He puts his hand on my obtusely formed left shoulder. "Son, I've been thinking of doing this for sometime now. And I know it is right. But I've been afraid."

"We haven't time—"

"No, no. I've been selfish. Here, son... I'm sorry. You'll understand soon enough, and I know you'll do best for us all." I hear him pull something out of his dressing gown pocket. What is he doing?

...Father?

His hand still upon my shoulder, I turn knowing he will not evade me this time, and I finally see him, and he is raising a needle and syringe containing some peculiar and illuminate purple fluid into the air between us. He winks at me, his face a gentle glow of purple light in the dark and before the scintillating fluid of the syringe reflecting from upon the hull of our green ship— the one I wish us to board, and now! He withdraws from a vein some of his blood using the syringe, and it mixes with the purple fluid and is gone. "I've been selfish, son. I'm one-hundred-and-fifty-four in a Tristar, and you're but short of your twenties."

"Father? What are you d—begag!" I splurt. He has leaned forward and grabbed me by the neck. The syringe, he plunges it into my artery. He... injects.

"Live son. And be better than I,—be who you are."

Father! He is so weak. He collapses into my arms. The syringe falls and shatters to my right. *Father! Father!* No, Listener, no. He fades. His eyes blink faintly at me. His body is so weightless as I hold him, as he becomes no more; his being disintegrates before my eyes into dust and light. A golden haze remains momentarily where once he were and then swirls, lazily, about the ship. There is a purple sting in my eyes as I cry.

Listener? Listener? What am I to do? He is gone.

My arms. My chest. I feel something move under my skin. What now? I—I am subdued. I fall to the cold marble floor, movement is not capable of me. I feel warm, gently heated from inside. As though again I am within that womb of heat, as once was I before the gaze of the Eye. My limbs and torso are contracting, convulsing. My skin crawls.

Purple light floods my sight and slides down, into me. Through the tall windows of the hanger in where we keep our ship the sun's first light lifts the darkness and I can faintly see around. I manage to stand and on wobbling legs throw myself at the ship's hull. He's gone. What did he do?—I but now lean against the hull of the ship and gasp for breath.

I look at my self in the ship's metallic-green reflection: and I see my father's face. He smiles. *Father!* But it is not him;

I am he.

The syringe. The purple substance. His blood. I realise what he has done. I realise his pain, self-anguish.

Society was too unkind to him. This world, he within it. He tortured hisself, his conceited nature but a clause to the destitute, unspoken mirror and roots of his mind. I will not make his same mistakes. Riddance with his work and mine, riddance to this identity he has left me. I will burn our laboratory and I will burn our home and I will leave this life. I will take to the skies in the ship that has begun this loop in the tracks of immortal memory, that has served to free me from the darkness of my ignorance. And I know, O' Listener, that whichever plane you so take me, I will serve you well.

No, hisses a voice between my ears. *You will take up your father's mantle and serve I from where you are.*

Yes—yes. Listener. As you have bade; I shall serve.

THE DEAD MAN

PART I

I've been dead for some days now,—only I didn't
realise it. My strength seemed unfamiliar to me. Winds
were not bitter,—they were only cold. Heat did not
burn,—it was only hot. In truth: I've never felt so
quick....

I've been dead for some days now, and I'm
beginning to rot. It was the smell that made me think
something might not be quite right.

So, today I went to the doctors; I didn't feel to be
in any rush; in fact, I couldn't have been rushed.—Not a
thing procured in me urgency, for fear, along with an
unprecedented increase in my strength, and resilience to
the elements, had died in me. I still see in colours, and
by that, I mean, I see right from wrong, red from green,
the bad from the wicked, the dead from the quick. Ever
since I have died a many great things have I seen... did
you know that people literally glow at the seams if their
soul breathes well, and if not they look dreary, and this is
why!—Did you know that? I look well. I glow, even
though I have died.

When they looked inside me, took x-rays,
performed various scans, they said my organs had all
ceased, and I shouldn't be moving, alive!, full-stop. Yet
my heart beats, they say. Once every minute. I've been

eating regularly, I told the doctor, drinking plenty of water. But I hadn't been excreting anything… they looked at me baffled, the pale nurses, the flustered doctor; I think I scared them, you know. People scare easily. A dead man telling them he doesn't go to the toilet, and eats, and doesn't ever feel hunger, only he misses eating sometimes… anyway; the doctor and the nurses were no help. If I had still been susceptible to fear I may have left their company as pale and shaking as they! but, alas, I was unmoved.

When I got home to my apartment, my girlfriend Mary looked at me worried and asked, 'What on earth is the reek following you around?'

I told her I didn't know, and I stroked her long, auburn hair from her eyes, and I took her right hand and put it to my chest. 'You're so cold,' she said and tried to pull away. But her hand was like a mouse trapped beneath mine,—not that I was hurting her, she just couldn't wriggle free. And then it beat, after a long stillness in my chest, after all the strength had drained from Mary's eyes, my heart, and she felt it, a tremendous thump that at once saw her shiver and jump; and her eyes wide, she asked, 'What's happened to you?'

And my reply was as this: 'They say I shouldn't be living… but I've never felt so quick.'

#

I'll take a moment to interlude and explain how it is this condition arose. I am a botanist, in my personal time, and I discovered a plant species I had never seen or read of, which upon my attempt to identify something quite peculiar happened: it disappeared. I had discovered it in a graveyard not far from the city in that I live, atop a clifftop and behind an old, old church that I had never, too, heard of being. This plant, among all the dead shrubbery, living and strong beneath my gaze as I looked out at the city far below and an acute distance away. The plant had dark purple flowers, a white stem, red roots. It disappeared whilst I was searching for reference points through old tomes, at home in my study, meek rays of moonlight dancing through the dark and piercing my garret window coldly, and in the air the plant, as it so vanished, left a mist, a vapour;—and that I inhaled.

    Shortly after, I fell asleep. The next day, when I awoke, I was no longer living as I ever had been.

    She doesn't know about the plant, and I haven't told her anything of the last few days or my experiences with... reality, and, now, with she being so faint, so feeble as I spoke that one simple truth to her, 'Oh, Dear, I believe I'm dead inside,' she hasn't taken it well, in fact, earlier this night, she passed out, Mary, my girlfriend. I love her unto my death, you know. I believe she's the reason my heart still beats (once per minute). That and one other thing: there is a dead man under my skin.

    I hadn't seen him until this very night, and it was Mary's surprise to see him first. I hadn't been out in the dark since three days ago when this all began, upon my discovering of that strange and exotic flower. It is to my own surprise that I have discovered an uncanny lair of reality beneath that of my gained power and seemingly complete resilience to the elements: when stroked by the moon's rays, decayed flesh and goldfish eyes of my former self come to the surface (a corpse). It is truly haunting, yet ever intriguing. Mary, however, was petrified. She dropped like a block of wood blown over in a strong breeze.

I picked her up and carried her weightless frame to our bedroom where she now lays beneath quilts, in warmth. I do not need to sleep myself, it is only an act I perform out of past habit; I await her awakening; I plan not to convey to her this truth, for it would tear us apart, I believe. Though not do I know how long I can keep this reality concealed that I now live in from her. Surely, yes, she will believe what she saw was a dream, or not even remember. But what when next he appears, the Dead Man under my skin?

#

She woke and I greeted her with a coffee, asked if she had slept well. 'Yes,' she said, 'but I had the most peculiar dream. I dreamt you had died, and were still walking around, and that you… well… you ate me, whilst I slept, in this bed. And there were people watching through the window, people with hollow, black, staring eyes.' I comforted her, for she was highly distressed upon remembering her dream to me. And it, too, had disturbed me, for whilst I have complete control over myself, and fear is not a part of my experience any longer, I could not but consider this a prophetic horror that may come to pass—and it is for her safety that I only feel remnants of fear, though not fear I would call it, but love;—however, on the flip-side, Mary is weak and she is prone to fearful feelings and fanciful thoughts and dreams. It is not something I will invest my own thought toward too strongly. And, to ward it, I shall maintain the control that I have found in my strength and resilience.

Truly, I am not dead. I am alive. I am in control.... I am quick.

PART II

They do stare through our windows, with black, hollow eyes. I have seen them now. Those that watch, that wait. They wait for me, for the moon and the dark, for the Dead Man.

—And he wants to play with them, he that is dead. The shrivelled and decayed I beneath the visibility of my glowing, eternal flesh. I have become quite a sight now. People stare at me in the streets. Mary is transfixed by my beauty. It has been only a week.

I have searched for another of the same species of the plant that procured *this*... God be good, this state that I now live in. Euphoria some people would call it. But I laugh at them, those that gaze and cannot throw off their attraction to me. Unable are they to look at themselves so, for the demons that cloud the mind, the heart. It is not euphoria to see all the many twitches and limps and sad, sagging faces, bulging seams containing inner, tormented realities of each beggar-victim passerby, each little lamb, lost of the way. I speak to my self now in riddles. The landscape of reality that I fathom with my mind I beg not want for words;—

euphoria, it is not in me whilst the world that I see lay dead.

No trace of the plant has come to me in my searching, even the graveyard and old church no longer stand where once I had stood and gazed at the city, far beneath, from. It is as though where I had stood was not of here, this world. My love for nature, being I a botanist, has not receded, and as I further this tale to you now, it is of my mind to leave Mary—at least, for sometime.

I believe that to know who I am, or, better yet, what I have become, I must retreat into Her sanctuary in the trees where wild things roam and fly and scurry, *Her*: Mother Nature. There are too many dark haunts and evil persuasions about me here, and with black, hollow eyes I see them stare in on Mary at nighttime; I worry for her; I worry for what I will do; I worry for the sweet smell of her body when at night I become a living corpse.

I should have left. Why did I stay, oh, why! I can hardly control him on a night now. *The Dead Man*, why, why does he want to eat her flesh? I shrivel at the sight of him, his glaring, grey teeth, bloodless gums, evil eyes. He is not I! He is a possession of that which is diseased. He who wishes to taunt me. He, who whispers to me, in the mirror everywhere I see, and in my head throughout the day: *You're going to loose her. She's ours as much as she is yours. Wait till I takeover tonight, maybe I'll have my way, maybe I'll have your way. You're dead! You've always been dead. They're all dead. Let us take over, let us have her. You can watch, enjoy. Enjoy the sweet smell of her flesh. Enjoy her with us.*

They crowd our bed now as we sleep, or as she sleeps and I lay awake. I am paralysed on a nighttime, due to my transformation, and throughout the day I shiver with gloom, never fear but just gloom. I thought I could overcome it, overcome them, but they are everywhere, and my search for the flower has proven fruitless. But I can't leave her here. Not with all those faces that stand now at our bedside, in the dark, pressing ever-closer. I must take her with me, into the woods.

#

'But why, Darling, why are you dead?' Mary asked me last night in a dream. I slipped away for the briefest of seconds. It was them, the hollow darkness that gazes; the smell of rot, of me, of them, it seduces you if you allow it;—and somehow I allowed it, I gazed back, I smiled, and then there she was before me, asking of me: 'Can you come back, can we be as once we were?'

'NO!' I blurted, awakening from the shimmer of my dream, and it slithered away, her face, the questions; dawn coming then upon the darkness of the skies; a rustling sounding behind the dark-purple curtains of our bedroom window. The strong and foul smell of *him* was gone the moment light peeked over the horizon and the black of night was fated to die. The Dead Man chuckled and I felt my mouth grin. Back to sleep, he says in my mind. The smell of rot is only faint throughout the day. Others that are not myself don't seem to notice it. A strange, sweet scent comes through too strong.

'Mary, Mary, wake up.' She stirs gently. 'We're going on a trip, Mary. Where they can't find us.'

'Who? Where—what time is it?' Questions again. I can't answer them. I'll have to lie.

PART III

She never fully awoke that morning I told her we were leaving, something kept her from wakefulness, and I had to carry her.

I brood on the cliff edge that over looks our city, the place where I found that drat flower, where the graveyard had been and is now gone, where an old church had appeared in my wandering and is, too, gone, gone as the flower, gone as my mortality. She sleeps, Mary, and she stirs lightly, only lightly now,—her slumber has grown heavier each day. They do not follow us anymore, not out here, away from the city, the shadows which hound; we are safe.

A dense tangle of woodland lives up here, I tell you; it moves. Somehow, upon carrying Mary out of the city under the partial cloak of twilight, before the approaching of dawn, bounding as I were, I came upon a cave deep in the tangle of trees and shrubbery here aback and above the city, without thinking, far in the woodland, as though I were guided by the leaves and twigs and pointing branches, shifting streams! arhh. What trickery I feel at play upon myself. And it is in this cave of which I speak that Mary, with few supplies that I hurriedly packed before leaving, slumbers, and her sleep grows heavier, and her stirring has become so faint over the course of the week we have spent hidden that I sometimes worry she is without breath and is dead;—a corpse for the *corpse man* inside me. But they don't crowd us anymore, *his* kind…. It surely is a funny prospect to have gained such godlike stature, resilience, strength, beauty, to be kept alive, consoled by your former and decaying self. I wonder now, being where I am and able to ponder at great length these things of my newly found existence, if he will simply rot away, the Dead Man, be taken like dust in a midnight breeze as I sit beneath the moon and her rays; and I wonder then if I, too, will perish with him. But, but Mary—

'She's ours you fool,' I hear him say.

'Leave her be! She but slumbers, and is too fair for the likes of you,' I blare from the clifftop.

'SHE'S OURS YOU FOOL,' again he mocks, but this time he's laughing with my voice and his chuckling is like the gnawing of mice within my ears, and his words were hollow as he spake with my tongue, and above me I notice the darkness settling upon twilight, like a crown. He is me now, and I am him. (Though, it is I who retains control. He but mocks, becoming me by appearance of flesh and voice… and feeling.) How I want to devour her, her sweet flesh. How he goads me.

—I, I must hide.

#

The baying of hounds follows I, he within my mind, out there, all night.

I tried to hide from her.

But it was like he was tricking me,

confusing me as to which way I had previously trod…

and then there we were. Together, outside the cave, he and I. And the moon's revealing light, well, the rays never left my skin. And I can't say why,

or how! but they were drawn to me through the darkness and shadow, and when I stumbled into Mary's cave, half-filled with excitement, drooling at my mouth, half-horrified, screaming internally, the moonbeams, they followed me,—keeping he revealed and gruesome atop my flesh.

I struggle now even to say what it is I have done; for I dined on Mary last night! and I wish now ONLY TO TAKE MY OWN LIFE;—if take it I can.

#

I've tried healing her, with the golden glow of my immaculate flesh but, alas, it has not worked. It is only her left leg I devoured, and still she slumbers, still only faintly stirs. 'If only I could find that drat flower,' I tell myself. But it is no hope. The church. The graveyard. The flower. They are all gone.

But Mary lives. And something in this woodland is looking for me; I feel it, like I feel the pain of my love, the inoculation of my evil deed unto her; the flesh in my gut of her leg that I digest; her sweet smell loose within me, intoxicating all the more as it flows through my veins. She rests in my arms, this very moment, and the sun sets over our city beneath us, we, atop the cliff's edge, the electrical blink and glow, far beneath the falling darkness, of winking car lights and solid street lamps, illumined windows of flats and houses, pubs and shops, our distant, lost city, gazing up sympathetically.

I pray tonight someone will come.

#

He holds her. I chuckle. He drools. I stare. The moonlight rolls over our skin, and his reek fills the air.

Mary is stirring, as though she senses him,

and I cry,

I cry and I chuckle.

Hahahahahaha. I'm going to rip her throat out, aren't I? That's what he's telling me. '*Devour her, and she'll be with you forever. Devour her, and she'll taste sweet alway.*'

Suddenly I'm blinded. I can't see her, see anything, myself. Oh, I feel her in his arms, my arms, his dead flesh. I smell her still. We drool together, I and he, but neither of us can see. My first thought was of the moon, *Her rays blind me!* I think. But it is not so. The light that blinds is not quite silver, not so pale as the moon had been, but golden and bright and hot. 'Mary?' She spoke! I heard her. 'Mary?' I ask again. Footsteps approach from behind. I cannot move. He is chuckling.

The smell of my decayed self purges into the night, and I feel him, the Dead Man, leave me; there is a figure at my back; the light is blocked; all becomes cold and one word eases me from out of consciousness; sensation slipping, I can no longer narrate; for the one, long, delicate word which is spoke:

93

'Sleeeeep.'

PART IV

I wake and it is daylight, only the day is filled with a paleness. A pale, white light. I feel hot to my right and cold on my left, and when I look up, noticing simultaneously that I am in the graveyard that I thought evermore lost to me, I see in the sky, a dark, dark black sky, west, over the city which is shrouded by a grey fog, the moon, bright, luminous, silver; and to my right is the sun, the heat, his golden rays awakening my eyes and my sense. The moon seems so distant yet large, and like an eye I feel her gaze, and I sense something, someone. Ahh! the moon pierces with such coldness; someone is there, about, but *where*; 'Reveal yourself!' I scream.

The grass is white, tree barks black in the distance to my right, leaves red and orange, and the church and the gravestones appear like shadows and spectral light; the figure at my back?; as for the Dead Man, I think, he's gone....

'I have concealed him for now,' I hear a soft voice heave over me. 'Who are you?' I ask, the pale mixture of daylight suddenly too bright for me to see. 'I am Her. I am He. I am but a wind. An echo of your soul. The cry of your mind. I have set you free.' 'And where is Mary?' I blurt. 'Your Lady is safe. I have concealed her.'

Concealed? I think, concealed? '—And she is safe, she is well? I—I ate her leg. Have you healed her?'

'Yes.'

The overpowering daylight recedes like a mist, and again I can see, but the figure whom was standing at my back is gone. I am alone.

#

Wandering the woodland, I have found not an answer. The city I dare not go near, for the ghouls I left behind there I have heard wail on mysterious winds that carry high and over the fog that conceals even the tallest of buildings, and I would not lure them to me—for her sake, Mary's. Every time I have attempted to search out our cave, to search for her, back here I have ended; the woodland plays tricks on me, I know this now. The grass is white and the trees black, and when I wander through it's corridors, an orange-red roof of leaves atop me, waving hands of black twigs and branches leering about me, I am misguided and streams, rivulets, bushes, rocks and boulders, strangely bright and coloured gems buried in the earth, the same trees, corners, paths, roots!, all appear to mock me, dancing about me, turning and turning until again I emerge into the open of this graveyard, where the church seems to be in my waiting; bells I hear ring when I am in the woods, and the front doors of the church are swung wide open—though, it is dark inside and I hear no noise but for the pull and call of a wind that rustles at the open doors and breaks at my back like the snapping of branches high in trees, when it is I stand before the church, and I peer in.

I do not wish to comply with the forest. I have resisted entering the church, so far. I resist this whole damn place! But it has been long now, and as I do not tire, as my body is seemingly resilient to all forms of chaos, I but the observer to action and reaction of my environment, I have become tiresomely bored, frustrated; yet I LONG for Mary, to find and embrace her. Where is she? Oh, Mary…. What have I done?

I enter the church as the sun watches from over the forest and the moon hides.

#

The pews were all filled. Ghost-like occupants with black, hollow eyes. A priestess stood before them all, upon a pulpit of gnarly wood. She was clad in a white gown, semi-transparent, so that a large and shapely bosom peeked out, her nipples staring through the garment, erect, dark, like fleshy-purple eyes. Her hair was black. Her face, her skin, pale. With long, delicate fingers she rasped sharp nails against the sides of the pulpit. She was a gainly figure, both elegant and intimidating.

From overhead glared a purple sea of light, half-dark, staring and flowing, ethereal and very much alive. The creatures in the pews all began then to hush one another, although none had been speaking. And she spoke, the priestess in the gown, the priestess with her so-very-shapely bosom so revealed, a pale priestess with gold in her eyes.

Her words were but a whisper. The whisper filled the air. The sound was not a language but a noise that soothed and invigorated. She withdrew a stick of wood from behind the pulpit and pointed it at me. The pews melted into darkness and the purple sea of light raged with hot fires overhead. And before me she produced herself, gliding through the air, and naked was she then, her stick by her side, her face coming to press close to mine, her long black hair cascading down my shoulders; and I saw that I was naked, and beneath us lay water and its surface was solid under our feet, and around us was complete darkness, the sea of purple but contained to a hole high, high above us.—We were at the bottom of a well, and beneath our feet, in that water, the Dead Man could be seen weeping.

I saw his eyes, and he saw mine. He raged his fists against the surface that entrapped him. The priestess drew me nearer her flesh then, so close that all I could do was smell her, and she embraced me. I felt then aroused,—strangely so. Intoxicated, I ravenously felt, and she stroked my face. Her mouth opened to mine and she breathed out as I breathed in. Her eyes illuminated my own with their golden allure; and I was outside, and the Dead Man was gone from beneath I, the priestess gone from embrace, the church gone from the graveyard; and the drat flower was in my hand!

Heat and cold merged in a terrific wind overhead. I saw the moon colliding with the sun. A darkness opened its eye therein, thereby the sky; a purple sea of light rained with a rain that was not there, for I could not feel it but see; and I felt then the truth: I was beneath a well, still!, and in the black hole of the sun and moon gazing down I saw her laughing, the priestess. 'Mary!' I cried, the flower in my hand crumbling to dust.

I know only one thing, now: the Dead Man is coming.

PART V

Wherever I am, it seems an altercation has arisen. Fear has sprouted in my heart and I feel the Dead Man as an equal entity here. Could it be, that for we are separated, that the fate that is each ours be pitted against one another. I must prevail against these circumstance, and at whatever the cost, I must prevail for *Mary*.

The sea of purple light swirls overhead, about the hole of darkness that is the sun and moon aligned (a portal, I believe, I somehow passed through to be here). And where was the church lay a staff I have collected. It is taller by a foot than myself and is forked. It is a meek yellow. I feel its pull, like it were a compass, if you wish, and I must follow it;—for Mary's sake, I know this. I am where he, the Dead Man, is concealed, and Mary is our prize.

#

Oh, I would have proclaimed myself LOST! if not was it for the guidance of the forked staff; to a river it has seemingly delivered me. I have crossed a waist-high water, and now I stand beneath a tree of a grey bark, deciduous, and with berries. The berries are red, and on their base is a pentagram. It is a Rowan, the tree. I ate some berries, and I pray to God for protection from the beastly nature of the man that has parted from my flesh, having I become corrupted with fear. I will, I swear, vanquish he, or die. And Mary, know that whatever outcome, though I doubt you hear these words, I fought, all for you; whilst all else could be felt to be falling away from me; you remained; my heart remained.

#

Like a joke, *hahahahaha*, that flower, that drat flower has grown before me! I have plucked it, however. It might serve me yet.

He's coming. He's coming. Oh, adrenaline, the fear, the anxiety. I do not know how we will do battle. I know my strength and resilience is yet with me, and this staff.... But he, what do I really know of him?

Movement in the density of woodland. Creatures rustle the forest's arms. Many steps, many feet. Overhead the black hole glares, and I glance therein the sight of golden eyes, and they say to me: 'Use the staff.' I walk to the water's edge. And without thinking, I have plunged the foot of the staff into the river, until no longer the staff stands in the air but somehow has submerged deeper than the prior depth of the river that through I had waded, even; the staff is gone.

I have nothing now and he approaches. Arhh. The wretch. He, I, my dead self. And what is this? With him comes a legion. The hollow eyes, black of stare, they are his. They surround him, thinly before him, masses aback him. Transparent, I see through them, their ghost-like bodies, as they glide, but I fear them not. 'Dark Ones, I beckon, follow this prowler of the Dead Lands not! For his fate will be yours, and I cannot help but cast you down with him—if so it be I should not fall against him. Stand with him not, I command you!'…They leave his side. What is this? …But, he has not faltered, his steps are true, his dead face glares with envy. He wants my life as much as he wants Mary's flesh. The fiend shall have neither!

'She is already mine,' he says from across the river.

'Fool! I will not believe your lies.'

'Oh, but you do. You're scared. I feel your fear, now.'

'Enough. You will not prevail against I.'

'*Oh, but I already have.*' He raises both his arms, and the white grass, on the side of the river that he stands, sets alight, becoming blue flame, and the black trees in the forest grow magnificently tall behind he, until I cannot see an end to their height. 'You think she is helping you? The witch? She is not. The elements are not. The trees are not. And that staff will not,' says he, the Dead Man; his skin is vulgar and his voice hollow and deep, grating. I face the corpse of my former self as death it endeavours to bring me. I face the decaying of death; and I shall face it alone.

'Then see it done,' I call from across the river. 'Cross this water if you can.' I smirk.—A flicker of confidence tells me he is powerless before the flowing water and its width between us.

…He, he is not powerless, at all. He has taken to the air! The blue flames rise with him. Over the river he glides, and begins then he with mockery, that harsh laughter, hollow, deep, grating on my nerves. Curse him!

Curse him!

PART VI

My heart. The fiend. I thought myself invulnerable. How mistaken was I. He has glided toward me. And I did not move, and yet, *still* I refuse to surrender, even now! He has torn it from my chest whilst it beats. Oh Lord, God, help me if ever I can please you. Help me, before I fall in defeat.

The staff. There is still the staff! Rise, damn you.—RISE. RISE. RISE. The waters tremble. The staff, Lord, it IS rising. And he hasn't noticed. Its white brilliance, never before did it shine like so. He becomes trapped. Its light suffocates him. I see him drown with fear. He is gasping, unable to speak, unable to cling to his breath. The darkness pours from out his eyes. Winds churn. The blue flames over the white grass fall. Dust glides along the river's surface.... Lord, he is gone?, you vanquished him.

I fall to my knees.—*Mary? Mary?*

PART VII

'So, where's this flower you wanted to show me, Hun'?'

I'm in the graveyard. Mary is with me. *The flower?*

'Is everything alright? You look quite pale, Dear,' she says

'Yes, yes. I'm okay. Are you?' I grab her and look into her eyes. Her hair falls over her face and she smiles. I can't see her, but she's smiling. I feel scared, suddenly terrified. The flower is in my pocket. I pull it out. 'It's here. I had it here, all along. I must have forgotten—'

'Oh, I've never seen such colours.'

'Mary, come here. Follow me, please. I want to show you something else....' We walk to the cliff's edge. There is only the graveyard, no church, and the sky is a darkening shade of blue. The sun has already set. The city is slowly illuminating far beneath and away, street lights growing brighter as the darkness descends. 'Mary,' I say as I turn to her face. I raise the flower in my palms, and as she watches, I crumble it, and its mist arises, but before she can breathe, before it infects her, or even myself, I lean toward her and I kiss her.

'Where did it go?' She asks.

'With the wind, Mary.'

The moon is full and her light cold, soothing, and the darkening of twilight makes Mary's green eyes gleam like strange fires through strands of her auburn hair. 'I've forgotten how it looked, the flower,' she says, and smiles, contented.

EVIDENCE OF THE BLACK ANGEL

Not so long ago I began having dreams, quite like old and forgotten memories. I would awaken and forget ever having fallen asleep. I know not where I am, even now, or *who* anymore I am, the date, time, and upon each awakening this has been consistent. I know I cannot be sure if this reality here is a concoction of outside devices, of my own mind contained somewhere under incubation, or if this constant awakening is reality as reality has somehow, for reasons unknown and fumigated, come to be.

The dreams came to me fractured. Bit by bit, I had the pieces of a story; a tale nightmarishly grown, and only accountable after awakening. If I awoke night or day I would not know, *do not know*, for I am confined in a room of bare and black walls filled with the steam of mine own hot, stale breath I miserably each time gasp upon awakening; and, of course, the memories themselves, mockingly there to greet me each time I come 'back' to consciousness,—a new fragment of a long and distorted chain, a dream-story I have been spun. It is as though no divisible seam at all exists between that of my waking moments and the flow of these memory-dreams, as though I never once fell asleep and only ever do I wake, gasping, knowing more, unknowing of when again I will be submerged into darkness, for to gasp again the stale air of this room; but now I am awake, and that unendingly so!

I have the full story. All of its traits are intact! I have not awoken for sometime now, remaining in this room of darkness, conscious as the memories whirl and spiral in my mind's eye. And, consequently, *delightfully!*, in this room where I am trapped, with no windows to see light of day or moonbeams of night, a table—which I can only classify as being spectral in material—made of dust adrift shallow beams of a strange and non-perishing light—has appeared centre to the room I am confined, with a quill, ink, ample parchment, and one flickering candle to illumine my purpose. So, here I am, moved from a steaming, stale darkness to a meek and clear light.

My breath has clung to the walls around me, no longer making I or the room hot, nor hard to breathe, for the cool presence of this light. The dark wavers around the candle, flickering, and impatiently, that I should fulfill the duty of remembrance and embalm this tale. The story is complete and no more comes to me now; and how I fear all will be lost, taken away, the light and all!, I, consigned forever, consumed by the incubating darkness abound solid walls which surround me without corner, a floor without level, ceiling without strictness. If I do not detail with words in ink to the materialised parchment before I, what will become of me?, lost, lost, in the belly of Mammon, I will not have it.

With quill to parchment, while the light still lasts! let me dispel the fragments to you, and hope, solemnly, that you are not the perpetrator of my confinement or the master of these 'dreams', and, that if you are, and it is your belly in that I am held, or your devices which subdue me, that you do not hunger insatiably, and my efforts congeal with the sense of humour you posses, you wretch. Hear me, Mammon, perpetrator!

This writing you witness now before you, my delightful friend, is from my seeming memory unto you. This text, these words before your eyes.... I feel my mind slipping away as the light flickers; I must not hesitate in the telling of the dreaded happenings I have witnessed. The light must remain lit, my words scribed,
—for love of eternity!

It begins like this—read closely now, *closely!*—a letter is read aloud in darkness by a male voice, few in years, quake, unsure, fast, as, beaming bright lights dissolving the abyss from whence these words outwardly echo, a colourless countenance of memory swirls into being.

"Dear Person of Importance," the voice spoke, and then the light, and all is made clear, "this letter written to you is in response to your proposal regarding '*The Evidence*'.

"In the body of this letter you will find attached your copy of the suspect's handwritten testimony, as promised. This is the only surviving written document from the suspect's hand. It exists along with several eyewitness testimonies, two autopsy reports of electrified victims (one dead beforehand, who had already undergone an autopsy; we shall be sending both the reports), photographs of a small attic-room where the roof has fallen in and the walls bear hieroglyphics of unknown origin; a collection of burnt, illegible books and various instruments having survived a singular and concentrated storm.

"Eye witnesses attest to having seen a winged daemon flee through the collapsed roof of the building in question after a concoction of horrific screams, trembles in the surrounding area and a 'freakish' storm.

"If you are not the appointed person to receive this letter and have somehow intercepted it, for your own safety and the privacy of dangerous matters, we would advice that you stop reading now; for we do not know what insufferable ending this letter may lead you to. The villain at hand, so far eluding all rational capabilities, has taught us by the mysterious deaths of many a person assigned to this case the keen secrecy in which we are to keep in our pursuit of him.

"If you are the correct person however, then the suspect's handwritten testimony can be found at the fore of documents promised." The young voice pauses momentarily. When next he speaks, a tremor can be detected, ever-so-gradually growing in the pace of the young man's voice, and in his reading it is clear both fear and marvel to be present (but marvel not, I tell you! For it is pure madness what is read aloud).

"I have not much time until the authorities arrive. And so, I will be quick, short in these writings of what I have achieved late this autumn night,—'A Soliloquy from Beyond', let us call it.

"I am a scientist, and a believer in the Divine. I sought to materialise and reconcile the soul with the physical form. I believed that in doing so I could prevent all future bodily and worldly catastrophes—all malignancy and corruption upon this plane as it is known—through the means of my personal striving, and transformation.

"I won't say my ambition was wrongly placed, or that I have even failed, for neither is yet clear. What is clear, however, is that I must flee once I have finished this account of events.

"My ambition tonight reached the Beyond. I penetrated the Veil—let it be known. I opened man's soul. I reconciled physical form of flesh and blood with that of the unseeable dark and light! It has been done. But, for the methods I had to pursue, I know I will be hunted (and, when my transcended form is realised, hunted like a beast).

"In secrecy, with help of no other, I captured a man of sinful notoriety. He was a rapist. Murderer. A cheat and liar, he disguised himself as a priest;—surely, everything the good of men would shiver upon hearing and demand death or that long-drawn imprisonment be imposed.

"My plan was to use two such vulgar subjects. My first subject I have already mentioned. The second subject was to be, however, WITHOUT the breath of life. That's right; dead. And so, again, I searched out a man of sin, but I chose this man to be of a greater darkness than the first; for it was from his empty capsule I would bridge my hand downward into the fiery chasm of a nurturing power I came to learn of years ago in my explorations of the Tibetan mountains.

"I laid the first subject—the yet living man, sinful priest—unconscious, upon a table, and bound him to its surface. The second subject, the dead man, I bound to a table parallel to the priest's. I then prepared the instruments (gathered over years of exploration; through the plunder of ancient tombs) around my attic-laboratory, and in the centre, between the two tables, I placed a Neolithic portal of my own craftsmanship, of which I, the third subject, was to poise myself.

"Long ago I perfected the procedure of bringing life back to the dead. And this would be a key in the, say, soul-surgery that was underway. My findings were always unfortunate though, regarding the living dead. Always my subjects came back docile, and, depending on the nature of their being whilst alive, they would either come back rabid, an evil set agleam the lost and soulless gaze of their eyes, or wholly docile and radiantly smiling, with beaming, vacant, white eyes! Both were simply too unnatural for this world;—but there was a power, and I could smell it! SENSE it! Something I had long been discovering. A trace of the Divine that bridged in that moment between dimensions, something came, I tell you, resurrected with them through the Veil; and that is what I sought after tonight. A power only I could feel, beckoning.

"—The authorities will not be long. I must hurry.

"I believe the procedure to have caused a tide of energy, sudden fluctuations in the particle density of the surrounding atmosphere. For I stand now, my laboratory centre to a highly electrical storm recently passed, all equipment, all research and recordings scattered or destroyed, burnt or near-disintegrated—exposed to the cold chill and gloom of a night's heavy air.

"With the two bodies set in place, the living man stirring into wakefulness, I began. However, I am not going to share here in detail the apparatus more than is required, or the working of my procedures.

"The first step was to breathe life into the dead.

"The dead of my two subjects was fresh from life. His capsule was intact, merely he cold, clammy, pale, without breath or pulse. Strapped to the table parallel the stirring priest, I revived him to, with a method only I am privy to among mortals; and his eyes shot open and pupils shrivelled, choked voice immediately bawling, inhaling he greatly the air and gasping, beneath the bright lights of my cramped attic-laboratory. The living subject, the priest, stirred into wakefulness, and, unfortunately for my ears, soon began to wail for the sight of the horror.

"Quickly, the air of my laboratory was filled with the one screaming voice of a sane man and another—vile and growingly audible—inhuman, wretch! I gagged them both, lest I risk exposure prematurely to my desired transformation.

"Upon the Neolithic portal, hooked to the instruments about the room, I stood. And when it began, the dive into the Nether, the place I knew I was to visit, my laboratory, the earth beneath, how so it trembled....

"Winds picking up in a spiralling motion about the building I resided. Thunderous claps bellowed through the night sky. My mind, my sight, all earthly sense left I, TRANSCENDED I. Then darkness, like I was in a womb, dead. Shadows. And a feeling of great sickness flooded me, and I knew myself then to be vanquished upon a burning shore of Hell. Heat like one could never imagine. Fire and pain and wailing. A hand caressed me then, stroked me in its dark embrace, with claws that both tickled and itched madly, and I was made to scream, and gnash. The horror lasted for an undeterminable amount of time. Only a glimpse, I believe; (I do not remember it so well, and the time this experience lasted for feels unfathomable, outside of remembrance; a mere fraction in time is all I can recall.)

"When finally opened I mine eyes and regained earthly sense, my living subject, the priest, was dead. And my undead subject, having ripped free his gag, pitifully leaned toward me like a writhing parasite yawning with soundless, hungry jaws.

"My blood was hot. My skin ice cold. My muscles felt weak, at first, or at least stiff, and my stomach was filling quickly with great malady. Lightening had struck my roof I saw, debris still collapsing horrendously around I and my laboratory, subjects and equipment. I was knocked down as a section of the roof collapsed upon my person, but the blow did not injure me, or even pain me; for the pain I could feel was already too much, everything else was as a gentle wind about I,—in contrast, of course.

"I began to retch when next I stood. A black substance, like oil, perforated from my mouth in unnatural amounts. My body started to twinge. I fell to my knees, moaning, dropped onto my side, curled into a ball as the transformation consumed my senses again. When it was over, I stood up, and I could FEEL it all. It was INSIDE of me. The darkness. The light. All things eternal!

"I raised my left hand in the direction of my undead, reborn subject, a feeling passing over and through me; and a bolt of lightning struck where I had directed it! My subject's writhing, his malignancy, resurrected form was immediately silenced in one powerful, electrifying strike of which I had autocratic control. There is a power within me now, I thought in the silence of that moment, my entire body, my SURROUNDINGS, THE ENVIRONMENT. Like a muscle, I can flex my mind.

"If you were to see me in person, fear would have you. I do not look like a messenger of Divine Light. I look corrupt, I'm afraid. My left arm is a twisted matter of black flesh and of bright blue veins. My right arm has bloated to grotesque size and is of great physical strength. My hands have both grown and fingers become sharp, likened unto claws. Even my elbows have mutated, elongated: sharp ridges, inescapable edges. The rest of my body is like carved metal, hard, cold, most of my skin torn and peeled away, pulsating red muscles revealed plainly among black strips of a taut, burnt skin. My face, the skin of my face, however, my complexion, my features thereby, are all intact, unchanged, as is my hair, brown and long and thick—except, for my eyes, my brown eyes glow ever-so-unnaturally. And at my back, torn, ripped—deformed, as though they were never meant to grow—I have these stubs, these vulgar sprouts of wings!

"Scanning the ruins of my laboratory, I see that all my equipment is destroyed, my journals, my notes. And luckily so, I've hardly had the time to account this never mind destroy the secrets, the methods to my transformation.

"The authorities arrive. They are running up my stairs whilst I write this very sentence on scraps of paper…. I hear their hesitation as they reach for the handle of my laboratory door. I hear their hearts pounding. Police officers followed by paramedics, I see them in my mind.

"To the world it must have been utterly terrifying; screaming voices and then lightening strikes. The cacophony!

"I *feel* it *all*. The man leading them raises his gun at the lock. I stop him, a simple thought pushing them all backward down the staircase they've climbed. The deformed sprouts of wings flutter at my back as I imagine myself rising up and into the air. I can feel all the world. The pain, the glory! I am as an angel. Marred, yet perfect. Such *PRIDE*. But….

"I am beckoned. What is this? A voice calls to me distantly. A name on the winds…. TOWU, TOWU, I hear you!

"End," exhales the young man, gasping as even I have many times in this steaming and dark room without strictness of roof or level of floor.

Light breaks through seams of darknesses to reveal one large, squalid, dome-shaped room filled with bookcases constructing a vague maze. In the centre stands three figures, and in shadow stands another. All is coated in a despairing gloom, like that of fine mists found where the dead lie in their ancient tombs, the walls and bookcases, too, stood peculiarly webbed and heavy with shivering dust; and the one permeating light illuminating the scene comes in the colour red cast by the moon; from the murky sky-glass of this squalid library, I observed.

"We hope you are the correct person for this pursuit. Your résumé was intriguing. The evidence, however, grows more and more disturbing with the reports received akin to the unnatural events, and assailant, depicted by *The Evidence*. The rest of the evidence will be delivered to the address, as requested. Hopefully, your abilities and knowledge will bring light to the whereabouts of the Dark Fiend the world unknowingly harbours.

"We look forward to meeting you. Yours faithfully and in secrecy—" The young investigator looks up before finishing the sentence, irritated for having read the correspondence and Black Angel's letter, aloud, for a second time, and clearly, he is outside comfort. "What exactly are we missing again?" trembles his voice.

"That is twice, sir, that you have asked us to read aloud the letter you already posses, since meeting here at your desired location. *Please*, make sense and shed light on whereby you direct our thought," says a beautiful, pallid woman named Nexus through long strands of red hair.

"Caesar, Maybe *you* have noticed—being that you are far more experienced than your two colleagues here—the clue I am looking for in the text," retorts the man whom with they speak half-hidden in dusty shadows between the gloom and darkness of long forgotten bookshelves.

"So far, I've noticed that you've had us deliver here, not too far from the prior location of event's past, under the roof of a very old and abandoned library, filled with decrepit books and ancient volumes most probably like the kind burnt and illegible in the suspect's laboratory, 'The Evidence'. As for our letter to yourself, read twice aloud, I see nothing of significance in the body of it that should stand out, nor the letter written by the suspect hisself, that we haven't poured over meticulously, ourselves."

"That's disappointing."

"It is. Now, why exactly have you brought us here? Your proposal promised information, your name and experience means of capturing this… creature… madman."

The figure concealed in the shadow steps from the darkness and dust of forgotten bookcases, and lowers his head to better breathe in the three subjects before he, dark spectacles pressed tightly to his eyes, long brown hair cascading down his face. "I will help you discover this, as you say, madman, detectives."

"Well, what are you stalling about? Reveal your thoughts! So far you've had me read, what we're all already familiar with, the suspect's letter—and even our correspondence to you, which I can't see to be of any direct importance," exclaims the youngest of the investigators.

"Quiet, Adam," commands Caesar to his younger colleague.

"We haven't much time, Sir," cuts in Nexus, "the blood moon is upon us and, this madman, the Black Angel, has promised us a great catastrophe upon the night of the next full blood moon." Nexus looks serious, her eyes like hidden gems, green and hard and unglinting, her long hair angelically ablaze beneath the lick of red moonbeams.

"Towu," says the man from behind his black spectacles, plainly.

"Towu?" asks Adam. "We looked into that word, figured it a name he heard in his head. We couldn't make sense of it."

"That's because it's not a name."

"No, it's not. It's a sound, isn't it," says Caesar with a calm and uninterested air, as though he had known all along.

"Well done, Caesar, finally you speak your mind." The man in spectacles and a long coat paces back around an outcropping of bookcases, walking out of sight of Adam, Nexus and Cesar. "Towu is a sound. And from my work, my research, I have been able to uncover its source. It is the sound of a great energy, an energy residing in the hidden depths and framework of creation. Its energy runs through you, through me, through us all. Towu is as a black hole emulating all power. It has the power to draw to its breast souls, remake them, and give them eternity; once harnessed, such a power can be turned in on itself, utilised,—I believed."

"Come back out here, I would see your eyes, sir," demands Adam.

"I beg your pardon? How dare you speak to me with such insolence."

"Take off your jacket. I would see what you hide beneath, also."

"Oh my! What a curious little fellow, aren't we. Why, beneath these humble clothes I can assure you I hide nothing I would not share with the world." From out the maze of bookcases he strolls, his every step concealed in the shadows. He paces but close to the ridge between darkness and light. "I assure you, I am already undressed and stand before you, though concealed in darkness, naked. Now, have you brought my evidence I asked for?"

"Yes," says Caesar. "Adam, bring it forward. Nexus, help him."

"I don't trust him," says Nexus, "come into the light first!" She draws a gun and aims at their acquaintance.

"My, my," he hisses, and then two bright eyes burn out of darkness and a pair of dark spectacles are flung to the floor. "Now bring it forward," hisses he with a tongue like a serpent.

Nexus' and Adam's glowering faces sink into passive obedience as the piercing gaze of two marvelous eyes convey their minds. Nexus sheaths her gun and turns with Adam to drag from behind them two large industrial trollies piled high with wooden boxes, into the pool of liquid-red moonlight before their acquaintance still in shadows, and he raises a hand out of darkness, and Caesar steps forward and is shoulder-to-shoulder with Nexus and Adam, and they are motionless as together they stand.

Out of shadows strolls the hidden figure, and naked he is, and abominable: his hide is as of a burnt man, black and taut; his veins glow with an evil light, and his eyes entrance. Caesar is unmoving but for his eyes in their sockets, and he looks to his right hand, and sees the mark his government has given he, and he regrets, and knows his fate to be in the hands of a beast. And the Beast walks forward, and with a glance dismantles the wooden boxes piled high and assorts all the equipment from out them about the room in the scintillating light of a full blood moon. He next strips them naked, his victims, the entranced, the detectives he beguiled into bringing him all that he so needs.

And to his needs he acts, and Caesar is slain, and his blood soaks the floor as Adam and Nexus are lifted into the air, and the life is withdrawn from Adam, and he too dies, screaming in his eyes, unmoving, and all that is left is dust when the Black Angel relinquishes his grip of him.

Upward leaps the Angel, his deformed wings morbidly aflutter in the streams of red moonlight; and he hovers over Nexus, and she, cackling, has already transformed to the like that is in the Black Angel when lightening shatters the glass dome; and in falling shards she rises aglow, mutated, an Angel of Darkness, and together, with the moon bleeding in a starless night sky, they rise on grotesque wings.

Fire reigns from the heavens, and the image of my dream burns.

BEFORE THE BLINDING OF LIGHTS

Jimmy ran around and around, chasing a circle in his mind, pacing the reality that was his bedroom. He was going forever in circles, it seemed. *Trapped in this never-ending nightmare, this sick, induced illusion, hypnotism! of transitioning pains and fleeting joys—who put us here—I ask, WHO?* Jimmy wondered and wondered, but he knew not yet the Who that so trapped him, only knew did Jimmy that not then or there was escape to be found and nor could it be seen.

His world was one of pestilence and famine, of magnitude and fear, desolation and grandeur. He was to himself a weasel or an ant, insignificant and small. Some might have said worthless, immature, weak, a dithering child; but they would have been wrong. For Jimmy was none of those things: Jimmy was a raving lunatic.

Jimmy went around and around with his thoughts, wondering *who* had trapped him, tying tirelessly the maddening knot of his mind ever-the-tighter. He felt suffocated between the delirium of the world and the oppression within his mind. The escape would come with a great release, he knew, like a lid finally exploding from and tearing wide the nape of a highly compressed bottle of gas, or a volcanic eruption deep underground—a great movement of a belly of lava, discrete and unnoticeable, until, at last, flames arise to the surface and devour each and every one a victim, each mere observer spectator, each form and shadow of Jimmy's mind. Jimmy was close to a reckoning of this sort, and it would either conquer him or he it—but not that it truly mattered outside the glass bowl of Jimmy's life, for to Jimmy, Jimmy the Observer as opposed to Jimmy the Oppressed, and to the retrospect of Jimmy's memory from the distant lands of reincarnation; Jimmy knew that endings are to beginnings as beginnings herald their very own end.—Not that this knowledge mattered to Jimmy, he was far too highly compressed on this day that we visit him, as soon you shall see.

Like I have said to you, Jimmy's world was one of pestilence and famine, magnitude and fear, desolation and grandeur. Jimmy's world was rather a circus; of the insane, of the blind, the thoughtless, dumb, numb and perpetually bound to the whims of misfortune; his world had been perpetrated by those whom pulled strings from dark and hidden places and called themselves powerful and believed their puny selves so; it was a world full of ants, or weasels, some might have said, of great shadows upon walls and lurching fears that reigned with tyranny over the chests and beating hearts of men. Jimmy had no love for the boundaries of his world, the procession of order that ruled each his thought, or the shackles that dared to his face, ever they always clinking and following at his back wherever he went, to bind him to the ill and unbecoming fate that surely he saw as and believed to be his dreary life.

The plane on which Jimmy lived had long ago been conquered and ultimately divided; the spirits of the people separated from theirselves. People had become made of the belief that what they could make, and what they could make others believe of themselves, was what they were worth, and nothing more. All people were insane, or at least to Jimmy they were, Jimmy who raged against the cruelty of the world, the greatest lunatic of them all!

He stood before his bedroom window one morning, the morning of the day he had decided to finally go mad, and he laughed; an evil smile cackled across his face, illuminated by the dim, smog-filtered light that pierced ever hopefully the half drawn drapes and dust laden window of his dismally dark and dreary bedroom. The darkness of dawn within the deep, concrete jungle of Jimmy's fume intoxicated city began then to die.

They're all mad, he both said and thought to himself. *They have so much fear, so much hate, so much detest, likes and despairs! They rot away, bound to lives they hate, no love for themselves, for the spirit that each they truly are!* And he laughed again—finally having he learnt the secret and woken to smell the truth—laughed as hard as he could, deep and from his belly, so hard that he thought his throat might crack and start to bleed, but he did not care how hard he laughed, or what fleeting thought came upon him in fear, because he'd woken up that morning from terror-less dreams of nightmarish things, things that once had driven him fearful until he reeked daily of terror, but now he had seen them; seen them for what they were: loose things in his mind, shadows that shriveled before the light of his eyes. And when he had woken, back to the dream of the world he had so seemingly been bound, he had realised that the very insignificance he portrayed of and to himself was but an arousal of those things, now terror-less and fleeing before the open eye of his enraged, awoken mind. *I will conquer you,* he said, *Fear, Oppressor of the Deranged, Shackles of Fateless Insignificance.*

Strode he then bravely across his dank and musky bedroom, surging with the will to fight back, and tore open the drapes of his window to blare his eyes and the darkness of his room with the garish, revealing light of day.

Great beams of light filtered over the city, down from the peaks of sky scrapers and tall concrete buildings. Jimmy's window, being so far beneath all such great magnitude, winked through the smoky, fume ridden air from the abyss-like depths of his second floor flat. The sound of the world was coming now to his ears, and he opened up his window wide and let the noise fill him. *There they go,* he said and thought to himself, *collars on their necks, badges in their heads, name plaques where names need not be; Ugly! Small! Obedient! Fearful! Oh needy needy needy need. They think they need air to breathe, food to constantly eat, water, teas, coffee, soft drinks, liquors, all to drink whenever they please, be it thirst of tongue or thirst of mind. It will always ravage them; never peace will they find, never stillness or true-strength. Not whilst those collars they wear remain, or name plaques to which they relate stay clipped on in-place.* Jimmy cackled loudly out of the window and into the squalid, lamp-lit street below: 'Take them off!' he blared. 'Take off your fucking collars, you mindless peasants! Why be slaves when kings you can be! Kings!!'

He slammed the window shut, and regretted that the glass did not shatter. *Idiots,* he cursed to himself with both lips and mind. Jimmy was losing it. The pressure had built up for sometime now. For pressure like this, this which he had brooded, was the kind of pressure one of his sort and confinement needs in order to wake and call the morning ever a new day, wake and smell the coffee and realise it a mere incipient dream.

Without so much as correctly garbing himself or cleaning, he left his dank and stinking room and marched the narrow, long corridor of his small and bare flat. He entered through the sixth door down and into the kitchen where he stood from a corner and watched his mother eating her cereal and drinking the prescribed juice from the corporation for that she worked. *Why Jimmy, you aren't dressed. Why have you taken it off?—Your collar. Jimmy this illness has to go. We can't—you can't go on like this.* Jimmy sighed deeply and broke eye contact with his mother.

It is you that cannot go on. And you don't even realise it. You wear that collar around your neck, and you slave away half of the day to keep us here, here in this—this flat. And each morning you look more glum than the morning before, or as glum as the darkness that never seems to leave the streets so far below as we are. Your juice. Pour it away.

She scoffed, nearly half-choked on her morning cereal, again prescribed by the corporation for that she worked. *I can't do that Jim. Have you gone mad? I mean, why would I do that?*

BECAUSE IT POISONS YOU, MOTHER. Can you not see? That collar, their orders, the prescription of every item of food and drink, soap, toothpaste and clothes. Do they even let you go outside for fresh air anymore whilst you work? They used to let some of the employees that 'pulled their weight' go to the rooftop where the light was strongest and the air most fresh, back when, when I... when I worked for them, too.

Silence hung over the room like a morbid illusion as Jimmy's mother gulped down the half-remaining glass of her juice and then sat still and unsmiling in her chair, vacantly glaring at and waiting for Jimmy to leave the room before she continued with her routine. 'This illness needs to go Jimmy. We can't go on like this,' she finally spoke.

I know mother, I know.

When Jimmy's mother had bathed and dressed and left their flat for work, Jimmy got up from his bed. He too left the flat. And he didn't come back that day. He wasn't going to come back, 'Ever,' he had said to himself. Today was the day of change for old Jim. He would find reason, or meaning, and he knew where he would find it; he would simply follow his feet.

And so, down lamp-lit paths of seething darkness and stenches that rose from the curbs and gutters, Jimmy found his way to where all the people of his building-block world flowed for their daily duty of work and obedience. Jimmy had believed first that he was to ascend the tallest building in the Great Square where all the largest corporations sat and loomed. But it was not to be so. For Jimmy was distracted, distracted by something which moved in a long and dark corridor between the backs of two dull and ugly looking buildings.

It moved again, deep in the dark, and Jimmy was taken by his feet toward it. 'Who's there?' Jimmy called out. But no voice came in answer, only a movement, and a rattle, it seemed, like the dark itself had moved to make a noise, and for a moment, Jimmy thought he saw an eye wink at him; he walked into the dark further, staving from his mind the thought that the winking eye belonged to a creature with some terribly sharp and unkind teeth—a hound of the Corporations, lurking where workers ought not wander.

Far in the stumbling depths between the backs of these two grey buildings, Jimmy found his answer. He found the Who. The Who before the blinding of all lights, before and after and ever in-between.

At some point Jimmy's feet had disappeared from beneath him, and he soon found himself to be walking on air, moving without limbs, without flesh to touch or a heart to beat. *The darkness has consumed me,* Jimmy thought.

With a great wail Jimmy poured forth a noise from his absent lungs and felt the tracings of a body appear around he. *So I am still here then….* 'Where are you?! What is this? Reveal yourself to me!' The dark then beat and it pulsed, as though alive. A shimmering some distance ahead glided toward Jimmy as Jimmy stared, seemingly bodiless in the dark all around. It told him to wail, to cry. And Jimmy did, not as though he obeyed a command, however, but as though he had said to wail his very self, without a voice, but with the voice come from a great light, the voice of some ghost that was he; and the tears that then came poured like droplets of light from all corners of Jimmy's vision as a shimmering white pulse engulfed the corridor of darkness that Jimmy the Estranged and Oppressed had thought himself to have walked into and become trapped.

Before the blinding of lights Jimmy awoke. He was home. And though all things were the same, dark and rancid, musky and bare within his small bedroom, Jimmy smiled as he lay on his back facing the cracked ceiling of his room. He had seen, heard, felt, taste, but not could he describe to anyone, an essence so kind and becoming, distant and unattached, that the day Jimmy searched for the Who became the day Jimmy remembered who *he* is.

THE THIRTEENTH GUEST

Slightly audible over the chaotic din of polite conversation was a composition of Vivaldi softly playing in the background. The Host of this dinner party began to speak aloud and caught the attention of his twelve fine guests, "everybody, please do continue your affairs. Continue eating and enjoying the music, but *please* DO listen to me—for a moment's sake."

Noise around the dinner table began to subdue, except for the odd clinking of cutlery and the constant, soft playing of Vivaldi. Conversation, however, utterly became deterred and all eyes fixed somewhat excitedly on the Host.

"There's someone here hiding among us who is not welcome to our company. Please, my guests, do not be alarmed; for I don't believe he can understand any of us when we speak. But let us speak more quietly, my guests, as to not upset this—" the Host paused and pressed his lips together for a moment, "—this person."

"Who are you talking about, exactly?" asked one of the twelve guests sitting closest and to the left of the Host.

"I cannot say, for I do not have him a name. Seemingly, I am the only one who noticed him come through the doors as the last of you arrived," the Host replied. "Please though, continue eating, talking pleasantly, as I, myself, find this—the change in tone, the uncertainty of topic—to be quite interesting, if I am honest."

Three women positioned at the end of the long dining table and to the left began to giggle together. "Oh my, and I was just enjoying this company and the delicious food," said the smallest of the three laughing women.

"You have the most exciting gossip," said the woman laughing the hardest to the smallest of the three laughing women.

"Please, Ladies, let us quieten down; I don't want to upset this *thirteenth* guest with any too sudden a change in atmosphere. We've all already stopped talking politely among ourselves, even now, and he could become, easily, agitated, I do believe, lest we speak with hushed voices," said the Host. The Host then motioned the Butler over and whispered into his ear.

The Butler left the room.

"Who is this man you speak of so delightfully!" spoke the large, round man sat in the middle of the long dining table—the only man still stuffing his face with main course, noted then the Host quite distastefully.

"Like I already said, I don't have him a name. I know his face. And he is of a large stature." The Host rose from his seat and walked to a cabinet in the far right corner of the room, slightly exasperated from conversing over the same topic. He crouched for a moment before a display of wine, and then, upon returning to the dining table, he presented a bottle of a vintage and unopened red-wine to his twelve fine guests. Looking to the fat man still stuffing his face and expecting him to be the first to raise hand in answer, the Host asked, "Would anyone care for more wine?"

But it was one of the three laughing women, the quietest of them, who answered first. "Why, yes, of course, Generous Sir. Fill my cup!" said she as, timidly, she raised her glass into the air. The Host walked down the long dining table to the quieter of the laughing women and poured a small amount of wine into her cup as she covered her mouth to suppress her rising giggles. She tried the wine, nodded her head vigorously in encouragement, and the Host filled her glass to the brim.

The Butler re-entered the room pushing a trolley in front of him. "Ah, dessert!" cried the Host. Conversation flurried naturally up and down the long dining table and the music playing in the background rose by the butler's hand a few decibels. The Butler then began clearing away plates from the main course.

"Ohhh, what could it be?" asked the large, round man sat halfway down the long dining table.

"Jello," said the Host, with a wide smile. The Host retook his seat at the head of the dining table and watched intently as the Butler revealed to each guest their finely prepared desserts.

With all guests again chattering happily, almost vacant in their musings and tasteful talk, and whilst they ate their desserts, the Butler filled each of their glasses with more wine. The Host sat silent, watching the scene, not touching his own dessert; for he had such a wide smile and was filled with such grinning delight that he was beside himself to eat another morsel of anything! The Host, the very next moment, actually flinched and knocked his own glass of wine onto the floor by his feet.

No one noticed however, except for the Butler who the Host motioned over and mentioned something quietly to. The Butler bent down, crouching to clean the mess, and disappeared from sight of the chattering guests beneath the table and tablecloth, his large shoulders noticed briefly by one of the giggling women, and then he was gone form sight.

"Delicious, isn't it," exclaimed the Host. "The company we share, so… civilised and uppermost, one might say…" The Host's guests began to shush one another, as though all should be expectant of the Host's next words. "But not everybody here is civil, no…. My, we still haven't dealt with our thirteenth guest!"

Again, conversation utterly ceased and all eyes became fixed, excitedly, on the Host. The three women at the end of the table and to the left seemed increasingly more drunk, and the man closest to the Host and also on his left seemed awfully uncomfortable in his seat. "Ohhh, come out and dine, our thirteenth friend!" sang the large, round man through laughs and mouthfuls of jello, his plump lips delightfully red with wine.

"Please, keep quiet, my guests," said the Host. "You ought not spook our thirteenth guest, for when I did see him walk in—following the last of you through my front doors—I noticed such a dreadful look within his eyes, like he was terribly tired and could lash out quite easily, so much as you tread on his feet, or speak too loudly in your seats."

"And what kind of a look was that?" laughed the loudest of the three laughing women, jello flecked disgracefully across the low and revealing hem of her blouse.

"His expression... it delivered... the fearful fancies I can't help but align to a man quite lost from himself—if I put it plainly to you. He lacked… the moral code, say, like we so have, we in our civilised responsibilities and conversations to one another. He looked enraged, his eyes reflecting only the base desires men should keep hidden—especially so was this look when I saw him slip unnoticed and hide beneath the dining table and cloth!—" The guests suddenly stirred, half-alarmed, half still amused, and one woman yelped, "—please! Nobody look, and *be* quiet, my guests, for the love of polite solicitude… else you disturb him!"

"He touched my foot, he touched my foot," giggled the loudest of the three laughing women at the end of the dining table and to the left.

"Stay perfectly still. Everyone, please," said the Host. Then, leaning to his left, the Host whispered in the ear of the man sitting closest to him. The man sat closest to him then, almost obediently, slowly stood and left his chair, walked in silence from the dining table and room and through the front doors leading to a courtyard outside.

"Where did he go?" asked the fat man halfway down the dining table.

"Where I told him to go; outside, and to wait," said the Host. "He was the last of you to arrive and he was the man who was followed in by our thirteenth guest, unfortunately, you see. I have a feeling our thirteenth guest will follow him again, in due course. I'm going to ask something uncomfortable of you all now. Something in which you must trust. The man I speak of, the thirteenth guest, the man hiding under our table, he is dangerous—" The Host paused and looked at each of his guests and noted the looks of apprehension in some and of tedious over-excitement in others, "—he is dumb, cannot speak, must barely be able to communicate or understand our civilised ways, and, most importantly, he was smuggling a very sharp and long shard of glass last I saw him.

"Now, what I would ask of you all is that you do *not* dare meet his eyes if so you're given the chance, and that you be comfortable enough to sit in total darkness for this reason. And for the next couple of minutes— until it is over—I want you all to stare directly up at the ceiling and watch the pretty chandelier twinkle, as it will be the only source of light and I hope for you the reflected moon beams gained through my high windows as they twinkle and gleam off the glass of the chandelier provide you the much needed comfort in such a funny yet troubling matter. But, no matter what you hear, you *aren't* to look around, *aren't* to take your eyes from that chandelier; not until I turn the lights back on, at least. This you must promise. You can make reasonable sounds however—nothing too alarming, nothing far from the mood and resonance of polite conversation, please. He will most likely show himself in the next few minutes. I suggest you all avert your eyes now. I'm going to turn the lights out and then sit again."

The Host turned off the lights and at once retook his seat.

"It's so dark," whispered the fat man.

"I hope all your jello is still there when next we can see!" quietly laughed the loudest of the three laughing women.

"Be quiet, you're ruining it," chimed in another guest, quite irritably.

"Shhh," hissed two others.

"The chandelier is so pretty," said another, "the way it gleams...."

"The way it twinkles!" spoke three at once.

A loud knocking came from the front doors of the dinning room. The man outside, the last of the guests to arrive, had grown impatient and was braying loudly and ever-so-hurriedly upon the doors leading to the courtyard.

Everyone around the table but for the Host flinched when a scuffling noise quickly found its way past the only open chair—the chair left and pushed aside by the last man to enter the dining room as he had duly listened to the Host and left his seat to go and wait outdoors. The table was nudged sharply. Footsteps loudly approached the front door. Light flooded the room from the courtyard outside and the chandelier shone brighter for a moment. The door clicked shut and darkness then veiled the room and moonbeams were the twinkling entertainment in each guest's eyes.

Outside in the courtyard, a strangled voice could be heard. The guests became unsettled. The three laughing women all laughed nervously, and all of the guests seated at the dinning table became weighted with a shivering fear—like the darkness itself had suddenly grown cold and stiff and sharp around them. Thuds were heard outside, and, once, the door received a painful crack. Then silence, and the door re-opened.

The chandelier shone brightly again, darkness lifted briefly before a closing *click* sounded and shut out the courtyard's lamplight. The remaining guests began to wriggle and fidget in their seats as the footsteps approached the dining table, unable they to move from their seats due to the burdening fear and a spell of confusion twinkling over them in darkness from that chandelier above. The three laughing women began to snigger uncomfortably, as though all that was happening, the irrationality of fear that had so amply replaced amusement and joy, was nought but an unfunny joke.

And then the fat man yelped, like a pig given the knife.

The three women began to laugh hysterically at the noise. "Listen to him gurgle! He's drinking his wine, isn't he!"

A sound like meat being sliced hurriedly ran up and down the long dining table. The last words spoke over the play of music and cutlery falling to the floor were croaked in a struggle by one of the laughing women as she complained of someone tickling her feet.

The Host rose from his seat and turned the light on. He noticed instantly that all of his guests weren't looking where he had told them but that their eyes were fixed upon their deserts instead. He tutted, retook his seat, and watched his guests shamefully slouched and un-importantly limp in their chairs, heads hung forward, eyes dim and vacant. "*Tut, tut, tut,*" hissed the Host viciously as he noticed the red wine they had all spilt down their fine garments. "Have you finished cleaning down there?" The Host asked the Butler who was crouched and clearing away shards of broken glass by the Host's feet, scrubbing with another hand large red stains from the wooden flooring.

"Oh, where are my manners!" exclaimed the Host as he bestowed to his twelve fine guests a large grin which stretched quite horribly his skin and made him twitch with sharp spasms of delight. "Would anyone care for more wine?"

FIGURINES

I couldn't say whether or not it was a joke, but I held in my hands an uncanny representation of my girlfriend—a figurine no bigger than one of my thumbs. She had told me once, before she had left me, and then when she had returned and forgiven me, she told me what they all told me, each girlfriend I've ever had: "One day you'll hurt for this yourself."

But I'd never expected *this*, and what was she trying to do? Make a joke, leave a final signature? Would she turn back up in the car I bought her, come running back into my house and say again she loves me and that she can't leave? I didn't think so at the time.

But what was I to think? She'd up and disappeared in the middle of the night. I hardly knew she was gone till morning. No arguments had we had. And she knew not of any further indiscretion I might have made since last she forgave me for such or any acts. I had woken up, unusually early. The sky had still been dark, and I find on her pillow this, *her!* The figurine that says she's gone.

Pale blue. The figurine's eyes were pale blue, as was the silk dress it wore. Glossy marble eyes caught the sun's faint light and winked up at me in the semi-darkness of our bedroom. *It looks just like her,* I thought then, *where did she acquire it?* It even wore one of her dresses. There it was, another likeness I could not comprehend.

I bent the figurine's arms, pivoting them upward by their hinges, so that its hands covered its eyes; like she was hiding from me. I smiled. I got up from our bed, fully dressed. I had been pacing our room for hours, making phone calls that no one answered—not a single relative, not any of our friends. The only thing I hadn't yet done was search for her myself. And I wonder then why I had not already began to look, even gone to the police. This could be a sick joke, a game played by some deranged third party. *No no it is her,* I thought, covering up waves of discomfort elected by the dreadful notion. I reflected then on her actions of late, anything that might hail a reason for her disappearing, and the style by which she had left.

She'd been quiet, that much was immediate in my mind. It hadn't been a great deal of time since she'd forgiven me, you see. At first she had been extremely warm toward me, as if her forgiveness had been some defiant act against the world. But I believe that dream paled, for I felt in sometime—a month, maybe it was two?—that the warmness that she had greeted me with upon returning had faded to but a shadow, and I could not blame her for it. I did not try to rekindle the passion I saw so surely slip from her eyes and touch. For what I had done to her, the lies, was humiliating, I knew that. And she must have known that herself, come to see that; and that's when she realised that she hadn't defied the world, she'd defied her own self. I had not even apologised, and a part of me had never truly felt sorry.

She's really gone, I thought then, and a bitter, unusual taste writhed on my tongue as I stared into the glimmering eyes of her figurine. I threw it aside onto her pillow. It fell off the bed. *Clunk, chip, clunk,* I heard it bounce and slide along the floor until it disappeared beneath the cold iron of the bedroom radiator.

I hurried down the staircase, red painted walls a dark blur glaring from all around. I found my car keys quickly enough. Though the front door was already unlocked. I emerged into a bleak morning and, feeling my heart sink and a strange emptiness howl from in my chest, the sky glared at me with a barren expression, and rain seemed imminent.

I climbed into my car, a tall four wheel drive. I could already hear the engine roaring in my head, as though alive with my frustration at the cruel trick I had awoken to. But I did not mange to start the engine. I revved the car numerous times and finally then gave in; it didn't take long. All the earth around me seemed black, and the light of the morning sun barely seemed to penetrate a smoggy greyness of the skies above.

To my side I saw a shoebox, positioned neatly on the passenger's seat. And I thought it was strange, I thought, *She left this?* When I picked it up a cold feeling shot through my arm and a knot deep in my chest winced. A final parting gift, I thought. And when I opened the box, there she was. Pale blue eyes glinting and staring up at me. The figurine. *Either there's two or I'm going mad,* thought I, shutting tight my eyes and reopening them three times. But still she was there, minute and plastic.

Who? How did she...—my mind froze, thoughtlessness numbing the inherently felt confusion, after seeing the many blank, staring eyes and smiling faces peering from out that box. She atop them, them beneath her, buried and strewn in all different directions. Each lover I had intimately known, uncannily represented, their faces smiled at me through the dull plastic of minute figurine forms. Dresses I remember them wearing, some even in night gowns and other frilly things they had worn for me in private. 'How did you discover such detail of my past?'—would be the question I'd have asked her. But it wasn't her behind this act. I knew that somewhere inside.

I dug through the pile and went from lover to long lost friend, to relatives I hardly anymore knew. Figures of each my brothers and sisters, one of my father, and of my mother who I watched die in my youth; people I have loved and lost, people I have left behind. *Where are you? Where are you?* I cried into the box, my tears falling over the blue silk dress of my gone girlfriend, splashing across her cold, unfeeling plastic face and the many faces huddled around and beneath her.

The sky began to illuminate then as a slow light filtered through the grey smog. I looked out the front and side windows at the dark earth about. And as the soft glow of that morning's sun reached into the dark of our garden, I saw how they stared at me, the trees, like people watching, and their leaves remained still and did not blow in the wind.—The rain, imminent as it had been, never came.

DEAD TO RIGHTS

Knock, knock, knock at the door. The old lady rushed, dropping her kettle with a start, for the knocking at her front door. "Who's there?" she asked. "Open the door please, ma'am," answered a deep, male voice. "No no, not you again. I'm not letting you in," she replied. "We have a new agreement for you, ma'am. Please, I'll post the document through the letter box."

A single sheet of paper pushed through the flap of her rusted letter box and she took it in two trembling hands. "What is this?" she then asked.

"It's a new agreement, ma'am. It says, that if you sign it and so agree, instead of we having repossessed your belongings, upon your death you will donate your organs to our medical research centre... to help better the lives of others, of course."

She squinted at the words on the sheet, unable to read them for the lameness of her eyesight. "May I have my glasses back, so I may read?" she asked. "No, ma'am. But all your belongings so far taken will be returned to you in exchange for your signature on that dotted line at the bottom of the document you hold." A red pen pushed through the letter box. She took it. "The pen is free," said the deep voice through the door. "And all my belongings will be mine again and you'll leave me alone? You promise this?" "Yes, ma'am, that's what the document says."

"Okay then...." And she signed the document upon the dotted line with the red pen they had supplied and she gently pushed back the document through the flap of her rusted letterbox.

The next day, a loud knocking came at the front door. She, again, dropped her kettle and panicked, rushed to the door and opened it up. Two large men came inside her house without so much as a welcome, and carried indoors her couch she so missed. Next it was her television, and then her microwave. Her kitchen fridge was returned to her, and all her tea cups along with it. Her plates, her cutlery, followed suit, and when the men had done carrying inside her belongings, they gave her back her glasses, said not a word and left her home—leaving too the prints of their filthy boots.

The old lady felt happy again, peaceful, able to sit around and relax as she so had wished, now that all her belongings were once hers again.

The next day came as every other day came, and a loud knocking came at her door.

"Who is it?" she called from her couch, panicked and slightly spilling hot tea on her legs.

Knock, knock, knock at the door. And she got up, rushed to the door, and called again, "Who is it?" But nobody answered. *Knock, knock, knock* at the door. "Who is it?" she asked, quite breathless. "Have you come with my inhaler, you seem to have forgot it yesterday." *Knock, knock, knock* even louder at the door. Her heart began to beat quite too fast and she stepped away, ever-so-fearful at that knocking upon the door. "What do you want?" she asked. "I signed your paper! There can't be anything more!—Please, I was just watching my television and having a cup of tea when you came knocking at my door." *KNOCK KNOCK KNOCK* at the door.

She became very scared, backed away onto her stairs, afraid her door might just crack, the glass shatter, the next time they knocked like that.

Knock knock knock, knock knock knock, knock knock knock, they knocked and knocked on her door. And her heart, how it beat very fast as the knocks on her door grew quicker and quicker. "Please," she called, "you're going give me a heart attack and all I'm trying to do is sit on my couch before you came." She got to her feet and rushed to her kitchen. She looked at the fridge and noticed she hadn't plugged it in. She saw her kettle tipped over on the stove, and saw that she'd spilled a tremendous amount of water, also. Her cups and plates and cutlery were all scattered and out of their cupboards. She leaned against her kitchen table, struggling ever more to draw a breath, straining with her eyes through thick lenses to see the dark figures looming behind the glass of her rattling front door.

Rattle rattle rattle, the handle shook in the frame of her door. And her heart, it gave way; she felt her body tighten, her lungs collapse and empty out all her breath, and her heart beat a struggle of quickened, hopeless pumps. The handle of her front door turned and the door flung open as she fell to her floor quite already dead.

Two large men walked into the old lady's home. They placed her on the kitchen table. Already it seemed she was dead and stiff, and they hadn't bothered to check for a pulse. They placed a large work bag on a cabinet to the side, and they cut her open, and carefully they pried what it was they were to take from her old, fragile insides. Placed in glass jars all of her organs, they then pried her eyes from out of her head and disposed of her glasses. They peeled her skin, cracked her skull, took everything of her warm corpse that you would. And when they were done, muscles cut away and stored in their large glass jars beside the organs, they hacked up her short limbs and packaged her feeble bones.

All their goods gathered in jars, her bones wrapped in a plastic film, all placed in their large work bag, instruments used cleaned in her kitchen sink and put away in their place inside the work bag, they wiped her table clean of the blood they hadn't collected and stored in that monstrously large, bulging, stinking work bag. And when they left her home, they didn't so much as clean the floor of the dirty prints they had trod both that day and the prints of yesterday, they didn't so much as close her front door but leave a piece of paper nailed to its old, red frame; the document she hadn't quite understood, hadn't read, hadn't been able to, what, for the twisted lies—elongated phrases and sentences—bizarre legislation—the perverse order that she had so sadly been fed. (Oh, and they'd kept her glasses from her, too.)

FRAGMENT OF ZOUL

The heavens were a muddy brown and the land dark. All about me, like whispering eyes, lights twinkled in a black and bleak earth, and a wind wrapt around my feet. I knew not where I had been transferred by the current of Zoul, but my sentence was over, and released I had been.—Or so I believed.

Curse his indiscriminate sense, *Zoul*. My crimes were petty! And there he had cast me—a place that to my mind made no sense, and but only felt as though an extension to my sentencing. I stood as so, wits entirely dispersed before the face of darkness upon the earth— being it a surface not truly hard but like water or dense air beneath my feet, and a sky like a swirling brown bog, whispering breeze and glinting lights all around; and before me a hut of silver and shimmering light that at first I had not noticed for the peculiar sensations elected of my whimpering thoughts and observations.

The hut was most peculiar of all. It's silver light was cold, and with sundering rays it illuminated the darkness and split it into many fragments, so that before my eyes and inner vision flashed the spectral and haunting memory of Zoul, flittering in my mind as past observations sometimes do, and I did not dwell further upon the location of my being but instead moved forward toward the hut. I could not place words to the materials that constructed this shimmering, glowing dune or hut set in the dark earth, but it's cold, silver beams appeased me, and the wind that had wrapt around my feet, whispering over the dark depths of the earth beneath, uncoiled and slithered outward in all directions toward and through the glinting, bright lights, or eyes, that had first peered from the dark depth of creation, and then, in that moment, it was that I saw them quiver as watched they I entering the hut; and above, the sky ceased to swirl, and a flood of brown poured like rain upon the sound of my ears.

I met her then. The woman that was to bewitch me. Alas, however, she was *not* beautiful, and she had no grace. Her hair was old, her face pale, her lips thin. She smiled at me when I entered her small, pleasantly warm abode, her hut. "Would you like some tea, my dear?" she asked, and I nodded.

She wore a silver gown and she danced heavily about her hut then, whisking from one corner to the next, in search of a cup. "Where are we?" I finally asked, after sometime and remembering the alluring, confusing madness of scenery outside I hadn't expected ever in my time of observations to encounter; such madness, *chaos*, had come awoke in my mind for the need to comprehend.

"Why, we are inside the bride, my dear. Do you take milk?"

"Yes," I said, startled, confused. She smiled warmly then, showing all her teeth, and how white they were, how clean and attractive. *Inside the bride,* I thought, *what does she mean?* "Where exactly are we located?" Came the question then out my curling lips—half smiling, half grimacing mouth—I was both feeling angered and yet delightfully entranced. Her eyes answered me first; she fluttered her old and drooping lids, purple, staring irises and black pupils gazing into me, and I was told, by a whispering, like a breeze within the mind, entered via the ears, sensed by the hairs of the nose, that I was home; the only problem was, I couldn't find sense to ask another question or to think on what had been conveyed by her gaze unto me, for her eyes were that so entrancing I could not but see beauty teeming then in all of her hideous form.

She handed me a cup. Her hands wrapt around mine as I grabbed hold of the hot cup of tea she had made me. Her old, long hair lay warmly across my bare arms. The drooping lids of her eyes were firm, I saw then, and all her skin had tightened around a heart-shaped face that was pressing closely to mine. Beauty was in all her form, truly I saw, and a scent, like a rose trapped and forever having exuded splendour beneath the foulness of an ugly swamp in darkness and gloom, sodden with unwanted decay, breathed politely into my mouth. She removed her hands;

away she turned, rummaging then and stooping low inside of a pantry. Her old hair was still on my arms and I noticed that it had fallen off! and from her head had grown white, youthful hair, white and brilliant, shinning, long locks. Suddenly she stopped her rummaging and stood up tall, her figure slender and voluptuous and no longer broad and lumpy or misshapen beneath her gown of silver, and she spun around and glided to my left side where she lifted into the air a perfect egg, and she smiled from outside of my vision and cracked the egg on the rim of the cup. Yellow yolk and a clear slime fell into the hot tea, that only then I realised had been burning my hands through the cup—though not did I wince in pain but merely enjoyed the sensation.

I stood in that hut for such a time that care not I to share the truth as she had stirred my tea with a long and attractive white finger, the yolk of the egg splitting and swirling atop the surface of the pale tea, her flowery scents flooding my left ear and seeming to kiss my brain as the woman she'd become smiled at my shoulder. It wasn't until the tea finally grew cold, however long that took, *and I won't tell you!*, that my hands finally felt pain and I realised Zoul had not deigned to release I; and still, I am held his captive.

THE MAN THAT ALLUDES
a novella by Antwel T. Higgins

THE MAN THAT ALLUDES AND I

You will never know his face, The Man That Alludes. You will never see his eyes and know that they stare back. He is a ghost. He is a vision. He plays tricks to keep himself hidden, The Man That Alludes. You will never know him when you see him. You will never see him when you know him; for The Man That Alludes plays tricks on *you* and *I*.

So, for the purpose of this text, I am going to name The Man That Alludes with a name that you can call him by. But, please note, this name I shall give to him cannot be deemed truly real, fake, imaginary, or otherwise; for he plays tricks, real or not, you see, The Man That Alludes, and he could, at this very moment, be playing his tricks on us now....

So, for the purpose of this text, I am going to name The Man That Alludes after myself. I am going to call him by *my name*. I am going to refer to him as Antwel, so that when things begin to develop and we find the dark and the light, the terror and the beauty, merging together, you might understand, and even perhaps grasp, how the creatures of one's mind are born, where from they come, how they die, and, in the wake, *who* is left behind.

IN THE SHADOWS

It became worse when I met him in the flesh, but first I came to know him in my back garden under the fluttering shades of my many trees. He'd stand up tall out of shadows and allude my gaze to wherever he so chose, and then vanish, slip away amongst branches. It wouldn't be until moments later that I'd notice myself still gazing toward the place he had alluded my eyes, moments later that I would realise I'm still washing pots and I'm spilling water all over my jeans; moments later when that question finally came over me, as if whispered by him from across my back garden, to steal away once more my mind:

'Who am I? Am I who?'

The first time this happened I ignored it, but after waking up several nights later from a nightmare I couldn't quite remember, and in cold and horrible sweats, I found myself needing to go outside for the midnight's gentle breeze; however, when I stepped out the back door and walked some feet into my garden, I saw a shade, *him*, rise up in the dark and silent night air, there, again, loitering in the tree line. He alluded my gaze to a place nestled between the oddly marred and strangely withered barks of four pale-grey Ash trees, and then he receded into the earth like a breath of dark wind.

I knew then that it was he who had disturbed my dreams, and again I filled with the dread that had so lifted me from sleep, and under the moon's bright luminous glare, I found myself petrified, stiff and struggling with my limbs as I turned to flee back indoors. His whispering questions, nonetheless, managed to rasp softly after me, and throughout my kitchen as I closed and locked the back door: 'Who am I? Am I who?' his voice rasped across my kitchen walls, with steaming, echoless breath.

The next morning I stood in front of my kitchen window, staring into our back garden—like I would do, by the kitchen sink, washing pots from the previous day and watching his trees, MY trees, as time passed on by; all the while but muttering in my head the words of both a fascinated and decomposing mind: I am am I Antwel I am am I Antwel I am am I Antwel I am am I Antwel…. How such some misconstrued, chaotic stream muddled and seethed, spitting up through the holes and cracks that marred the bedrock of my waning, frail, and in totality, uncomprehending mind—all whilst I stood quite still, quite vacant, half cleaning pots, half staring outside and looking for him, for *The Man That Alludes,* for, as I have previously stated—and as we shall call him by—Antwel.

The burning feel upon my hands of scalding water tore me from delirium. Emancipated I from madness by sheer pain, instantly my lungs exhaled and I gasped, breath flooding me like a malevolent wind, as though I had just awoken, and hurriedly, from a terrible dream, having seemingly upon inhaling no remembrance of being stood in the body by the kitchen window but having been stood *out there* instead, in the garden, watching from a place between the four Ash trees.

I proceeded with the rest of my day quite unhinged, and then the rest of the month as autumn seemed only to grow more bitter and more stale in my mouth. It wasn't long then until I began to see him. Well... when I say see him.... Hm. Never mind. It is best I show you.

IN THE FLESH

I knew of his presence first in the shadows. I knew of him behind my trees. I knew of him as a question inside myself, whispering to the deep of my mind. I knew of him from within the peering dark of my back garden. He was a shade. He was a flickering distortion of light... he was unseen. I only truly knew of him, you see.

It wasn't until several weeks had passed and a dreadful winter come over me that I finally saw him in the flesh, Antwel. That question, too, that cold and burning question he had instilled inside of me: 'Who am I? Am I who?' How it froze my little self like numerous shivering icicles to the rusted underbelly of a discarded and toxic barrel; how he had so feverishly infiltrated my life, so intimately infected me. My fate, by this point, seemed simple. I believed I would either come to an end, icicle by icicle, fall and be corroded by the acidic puddles that lay beneath, or that I would I melt in the cold winds of madness and slowly cease to be.

It wasn't until I fell unconscious, one afternoon, however, that this winter inside of me developed. It wasn't until then that he first appeared to me in form more than the mere flickering of a shadow can to one's mind allude. I was in my back garden, in its back most reaches, where the light before and after midday could only be found in jagged wisps between shades of an ever-darkening darkness; in my back garden until I had ventured so far that I could no longer call it so, that is, but *his* woodland home. I had been climbing trees and searching bushes. I had already climbed such great a number of trees so far to see if I could feel him; sense him upon a breeze; glimpse him scuttling in the light of the sun over the tops of the ever-stretching woodland aback my home; or, quite plainly, as I surveyed with incessant and scurrying pupils, it was of my hope to catch him lurking from bark to bark, or sight him, low, gliding between the shadows that bent across the earth. I had become very worried that I would never feel him again, he and his echoless presence, for he had left me several weeks ago, left and burdened me with an imperishable absence. And that is why on this day, now reaching far past noon of when I speak, I found myself searching high and low, fervently, the woods aback my home for a trace or a scent of that horrible delight he had to me become.

One could quite easily have said that I was fraying in imaginary winds of the mind. But one would not be me, and only one, I, could feel the winds that stirred to keep in full-wakefulness the wretched creature of this grey existence.

So, there I was, quite steadily unhinged, climbing from tree to tree, far beyond the back-reaches that made my garden, of the fathomless woodland that I believed made his abode.

The midday sun had provided me with ample light, scouring away most all shadows that had pervaded the morn of my journey and procured me in that earliness somewhat rather uncomfortable, somewhat terribly slowly paced. I had gained confidence, however, in the bright sun rays that reigned from the clear winter sky the middle of that day, and I had made, thereafter, in my day's travel great haste. But, alas, woe it be to my troubles, for when the sun did pass the zenith in the sky, I found the shadows creeping up from behind me, as in the morning they had crept away!, and as the sun did traverse the sky and reach further and further its point of vanishing, the shadows, how they chased me into the unnavigable deep of his treacherous woodland home.

The disappearing light from the skies quickly brought a semi-darkness of the sort I had slowly that very morning trod my way into. And with the latening of the day becoming as a mirage to the morn I then did not merely walk or tread lightly but ran, frantically fled, you could say, travelling not into a lengthening recess of shrinking shadow but after the sharp and slender points of the sun's vanishing rays, jaws of darkness ever set, wide and vicious, at my back; and then I happened to notice, as though whispered to me from an ever-calm and watching eye central, within my mind, as though the astral figment of an eye had at once enveloped and opened before me, and my body and limbs became frighteningly stiff at the gained and sudden insight thereby handed down; it was that I had gazed upon by way of thunderous visions the until then unseen and neglected imminence of my need to venture back home through the growing tangle of looming dark paths behind; I saw a dark sea rushing through the forest and the sight of it jeered at me, that great eye closing and disappearing as the unnavigable maze I had with gaining want of pace travelled a winding vector through when cool sunlight had blazoned in my favour,—having I searched, climbed, clambered from high branch to lowly dampness of dark root for what seemed such insignificant a time—, loomed from all corners darker and ever colder, and as though a black and monstrous tongue desired to sample my flesh, taste the fear in my sweat, I felt a strangely humid breath on the back of my neck. I even fancied I could feel the ghost sensation of a rising slime slither up the ridges of my spine and a haze did, I will say, then ascend into the already panicking urgency that was, in complete disorientation, my pitiful, scurrying mind. The eye which beheld to me visions that had impounded I in the desperate nature of grim fear twitched and fluttered its lid over my muscles, I felt it so; and then a voice, quite like a tickle, itched in my head and it said: '*Run, run, don't stop till the climb!*'

Exhausted, delirious, panicking, I did just that, I ran… stumbled! more than I could run. Worsened and worsened did the vision of my terrified eyes with the brimming black cloth of night and of fear as a grim blackness seemed to rain overhead and bleach from the skies all light. More and more the sun's rays retreated behind the darkness awakening, and that icy spell of madness, of winter frost, that so *he!*, Antwel, had cast over the lake of my being the past several weeks began to crack and ring within my ears. I chose then in a severely unthinking and fearful state to clamber high the branches of a tree I had suddenly in horror halted by. I

154

would climb and reach through the tree tops, through the dark canopy, and find salvation by the grace of the vanishing light, *the sun*, by bestowed rays of that glorious, sinking face from in the distant belly of the sky;—it was my hope that should I find comfortable perch I'd be able to last the night beneath the face of the moon.

It was upon this tree, scurrying high as I did, a tree I found to be of increasingly slicker branches the higher I climbed, that soon it became obvious how hopeless and desperate my actions were, mad even, and how the higher and higher I climbed the more and more trapped I became.

I looked about from ahigh the branches I clung, frantic and scared by time and by place, when height I seemed no more able to ascend and the bony press of branches in my hands pained me so I had to stop and rest. I was shivering uncontrollably, clinging desperately, high in the dark and leafless unseeing chamber of a whispering, tunnelling wind, when the darkness glared up, and pulled me down.

Utterly stranded I found myself upon the utmost slimmest arms of that slick, slick tree, brandishing myself up and toward a faint wisp of the sun's receding twilight beams. Eventually, after darkness had thoroughly climbed to my perch, through fearful and unwilling eyes I forced myself to peer the looming shades beneath, that I might find safe footing down—or, at least, meet my assailant in the eyes, the terrible darkness that had followed I, consuming my nerves so that I had climbed this tree (—oh, how I hoped for a glimmering moment that it would be *him!*, his eyes that I met, my assailant, Antwel—*The Man That Alludes*). But nay, tangles of darkness—faintly, faintly I remember this now—waved and then weaved together beneath my feet, like the many limbs of a struggling thing. I thought I had seen a face, and then vertigo spilled into my ears as I leaned further and gazed more intimately downward, and my face hung low into that rising dark, and I opened my mouth and, dizzy, confused, out I breathed a breath of words: '*Who is there—is it you?*' But no answer came and my footing went awry and I slipped. I lost my feet and then my grip and fell a distance I care not to know, could not know!, for after the first four branches that walloped my head, striking successively all sense from my mind, the light from my eyes shivered once and vanished; and down with my heap fell a wet, a warm, a feeling, shadow.

No visions I dreamt, no sounds stirred me as I had lain unconscious upon the forest floor. ...And then my senses began to unfold from a strange concealing hold, and light scuttled into me from the unseeing, inanimate. As each sense came, and one by one, ever-so-gradually, I felt my body move and spasm and twitch. First touch, then scents of warmth and of cold, of earth and of rot, and the sound of a coiling, retracting rope slithering upon my ears, all this, dragged or scurrying, across the soil, dead leaves and over the protruding roots in the ground until my eyes fell open and my mind came screaming from numb, unfeeling darkness to the stinging chill of utter bleak blackness.

I screamed, a soar and dehydrated noise. Carefully I got to my feet, my legs weak and shaking, in the unseeable dark of night within those woods, and I reached out for branches or a tree's bark. The first my hands found were *wet* and *slick*, I remember.

Why I chose to climb that tree I can only ever know in madness!

It would have been hopeless for me to venture through the dark and to try find my way back home, but then, in a far distance, faintly, a whistling noise beckoned; I know I would have surely wandered through dark and winding corridors of his woodland home all night; and perhaps that is the fate I would have chosen had I known then what in the days to come lay ahead. Yes, at this point, I believe, had I known the terrors soon to stare me in the eyes and laugh, plunder my mind and sack my life, I would have chosen to walk and wander, aimlessly, unto my death, untouched by that evil, but know of these coming terrors, I did not.

Through the heavy and moist air of a mist, the faint noise came waving over bare and bony branches and past twigs, upon the coldness of the wind, and, hail a chance, I was bestowed by the sound of some dim and distant whistling a path to follow.

One foot in front of the other I walked and limped. I held my hands high in front of myself, reaching, clinging to the dark trunks and branches that decorated my straight path homeward. When some distance I had gained however, I began to notice a noise following me, as though the very shadows of the woods themselves had began to imitate in mockery my footsteps, behind me some, and not at a great deal at that. I heard four consecutive cackles, and the steps, they quickened and they began to *limp*, as were my own, every second step heavier than the preceding as twigs broke in a surrounding silence. I picked up my slowed and disoriented pace when I could hear, almost *feel* the presence of some shadow atop me and a shallow, panting breath, like that of my very own!, upon my neck.

Through the thick of Antwel's suffocating, dense and fathomless woodland home I hurried by darkness to mine small and secluded abode, guided by a whistling I could only then hope had set me on the right path. I began eventually to discover wisps of moonlight jousting inward through the bare and leafless branches above and noticed then that the whistling had grown somewhat louder; and as the woodland about me gradually became less dense, I felt a sudden relief in thinking that I had evaded whom or whatsoever had been closely following and mimicking the fall and limp of each my steps, the shadow that I had felt almost atop me; a joy came over me in knowing I was no longer lost but edging through the back-reaches that were my garden, for as density gave way to the moon's revealing light, I recognised some of the trees and shrubbery about... and then the whistling grew louder so. It wasn't, however, until I stepped out and stumbled free from the tree line of my back garden that I saw whence the whistling noise was coming—only then, it was no longer whistling, but screaming.

It came from indoors, from in my house! I saw and watched from aback my garden, pressed against the tree line where Antwel so loved to loom (my limbs frozen and unable to move forward), my home wail before me, wail and scream aglow with light before my shivering eyes, like the whole of my house had come alive, beneath the rising of a dark and full, precipitous moon perched as a conductor amidst dark clouds of terror and rain.

I've left open my back door, and all the lights on in my house! I thought, reassuring myself, and I limped hurriedly across my back garden and into my kitchen. It was there that my fears began to recede. Upon seeing the kettle furious and steaming over a fully blazing hob, I silenced the screaming noise, turning off the ring of flame beneath the kettle, and breathed a sigh of relief to myself, and, slouched against a kitchen worktop, in a mist of steam that made me both cough and grow extremely hot, I relaxed, as though sleep was to come over me. Such dense steam, I thought, waving the moist air from in front my eyes.

'Who am I? Am I who?' seethed these questions out the deep of my weary mind, and that voice, that voice that had spoke them, it hadn't been mine. It is he! I thought, filling both with glee and a deep cold at the prospect of his returning after so many weeks I had endured without him. And then my glee turned to ice and I felt descend about my room an unwelcoming, disgusted presence.

Questions stole over me in a frenzy. *Who* turned the kettle on? ...Was it *him*? Who, who is here in my home?

A slippery, echoless rasp breathed then around the bright yellow walls of my steamy kitchen, and I backed into a corner, startled and afraid. 'Where are you?' I screamed, and again, 'Where are you where are you, who is in my home? Who is home who? WHO?'

My bruised ribs had winced terribly at the effort of my screaming and pained me so that I coiled to the floor in a gasping, quivering heap for some moments.

It wasn't until I rose to my feet that the steam dispersed around me and all creaks and faint noises about the house came to a still. It wasn't until, after having limped outside for fresh air and having stared up at the moon in its perch high overhead, the pinnacle seat of the silent and watching night sky, then that my tightly wound nerves began to calm and settle and finally, having locked my back door and turned off all lights in my house, that I carried myself up the staircase to bed, in the calm of indoor darkness. Unfortunately, I saw him next, Antwel. He appeared to me, momentarily, upon the screens of my closed eyelids.

Nearing the top of my staircase I blinked. I didn't see him clearly at first, but he was there. I stopped before the very top step and I blinked three times. Slow and deliberately, I blinked to glance and see what that reflection quivering had been.

Eyes firmly shut and I saw the dark and all there was behind it. The first blink, slow, deliberate, eyelids tightly locked, I saw a reflective surface like skin on top of milk, like a shallow silver lake resting over black paper. For the second time then I blinked my eyes, and the dark, for the glancing of a second, glimmered with a penetrating gaze and looked back. For the third time I then blinked and he smiled, without yet a mouth to bear, without yet a face, he smiled through the dark and static ambiance therein of my closed and curiously shaking eyelids.

I knew it to be him, and it terrified me. Is he... inside of me? I thought then, suspicious.

I walked into my unlit bathroom, blinking and blinking. Beneath my eyelids the dark wavered and shimmered. Moonlight met me through the bathroom window and rested brightly, on my left, upon my pale-yellow shower curtain drawn across bathtub and shower. When I approached the windowsill and mirror perched there, I finally saw his face: staring back.

I felt my own pallid and dreary countenance pull suddenly affright and grow cold with terror and my eyes widen and grimace darkly, for his face, it was *mine!* reflected in luminous glow of moonlight and bright mirror's reflection. I knew it a trick, however, a terrible trick. He can not be I! I thought. He is playing me for a fool. Not a shadow or a shade is he this time, a whisper in my mind, no, he has possessed my image in a mirror. How humorous this was, truly. But he was not I, he had not control over myself;—for, as I could feel my face to be pale and cold and drawn in horror, eyes shaking and swimming with the fluids of dread, his face, how it glowed like dark moonlight fire, and his eyes, how they watched and stared without ever once blinking.

Unmoving and silent, his face jeered mine in mirror's reflection whilst I felt my own skin alive and crawling with terror, jaw trembling, teeth chattering, eyes wide, frantic, he but stood there and stared, his eyes, like dark reflective lakes by a moonlit pyre, holding, deep within a black and smoky gaze, the true reflection of my haunted face; and like that, it came about, that the image of my own terrified self melted over his dark and unblinking countenance. My frightful, crying mouth draped over his lips and he dropped his jaw in the gapping expression that was mine; lines and wrinkles webbed his calm face as he sharply, mockingly, screamed a silent cry from within the reflective surface of my bathroom mirror. His skin paled and slowly he fluttered his eyes, slowly and deliberately, three times to glance me!

I felt as though drowning beneath the invisible waters of a dark and long forgotten lake, for could not I breathe, for had not I exhaled the lung of air first drawn in upon Antwel's appearing to me in swell of moonlight and mirror's reflection. How he mocked me as I suffocated and paled further with horror. My paling and horrified countenance flaunted by he. How his eyes, raging with distantly burning fires, had narrowed so uncomfortably on me, his mouth now gapped and trembling, eyes fluttering in maddening frenzy, as though readying himself to burst out of mirror's reflection and pounce atop my horrified little self. How he then suddenly appeared to lose control... and forced a scornful smile. His taut skin began to stretch, as though claws or talons of some dark and unseeable creature was tearing the flesh of mine reflected face; and so taut and terribly did his skin in the mirror stretch until it began to crack and peel and split, and red and bleeding lines ran from his now trembling lips and up the sides of my reflected, pallid face. How quickly his ghostly skin dissolved into the bleeding lines that stretched and tore and encompassed the whole of that very face that was, seemingly, mine.

The last of this grueling portrait of he that I endured to see, before flinching enough in stark disgust to strike and shatter the mirror's possessed glass, were his eyes, glowing, yellow, fearful and drifting each to the sides.

The mirror broke into many pieces, plummeted behind the shower curtain to my left, and became lost, I hoped, to the moon's illuminating touch.

I exhaled my breath finally and caught myself upon the bathroom sink, inhaling deeply as my lungs ached with mine bruised ribs. I twisted four times the cold tap and splashed my face with water to sober my adrenalin drunk mind and calm the frantic beating of my heart. How dreadful I felt! He had mocked me, scolded me with fire in his eyes and darkly aglow face, MY face! Turning back the tap tightly I collapsed my legs beneath myself and fell to my right upon toilet seat and lid, my back colliding with the bathroom wall. Is he gone? I thought. Is he gone?

'Who am I? Am I who?' I mouthed silently, my head upturned to the ceiling, eyes closed, mind fixed on a humming black glare of closed eyelids.

I saw then next the slight thing that would reveal him, yet again, to me.

Upon opening my eyes and lowering gaze, there it was: a tear in the shower curtain, and the moonlight thus flooded the bathtub and darkness therein. That was not all of my fright, however, for two gigantic wings stretched then a shadow across my pale-yellow shower curtain, flexing and preparing for flight. My heart sank as those wings beat furiously the air, and up this shadow raised, hovering wings of despair, projected by moonlight's steady glare;

it was then through this dreadful tear that I saw him, Antwel, again; as moonlight's presence met darkly glimmering shards of Antwel's shattered mirror lying in that tub, a beam climbed upward through the tear in the shower curtain—a dark beam travelling by rays of moonlight undisturbed, and so it was he reemerged.

The dark and rising light that was he travelled inwardly the given moonbeam channel and met with the window's pane where it then stopped to pause and envelope the moon's light in a darkly ambient glow. Bathed therein this glowing darkness, I felt a sense of rippling peace come over me, and awe pass through me.

The creature's shadow I had so feared became then apparent before me in flesh and flight over the windowsill. The creature—oh, I say creature now for not yet have I revealed its form unto you—the creature, well, it was only a moth—an insect!, large and ripe as a man's beating heart;

how the moth hovered before the darkly glowing window pane, seeming almost suspended in animation as it's wings flapped ever-so-effortlessly to keep in flight. How beautiful those wings were too, and alive, as colours swam in them, a dark and a golden brown swirling one after the other, two halves to a puzzle adance in triumphant union, and far beneath the hues of brown swam alone, aglow in depths unseen, a hidden shade of a mysterious shimmering green that I saw reveal a pair of eyes wink like secret bright lights, or distant stars, a truth so beautiful, a truth if uttered one would demean it, the truth ever-serene and immutable. How such an aura for only seconds encapsulated those wings. Gentle and kind, fierce, loving, this creature's

wings before mine eyes, insect of darkly glimmering
night, amidst dark glow of Antwel's escaping light.

So thoroughly raptured by gaze of the moving
screens of those wings as I had become, the creature that
they belonged turned in flight to face me. Large and
black eyes shone in the darkness toward me,

What are you? I thought, and as though the moth
had somehow heard me, it's antennas coiled away, curled
up, shriveled, its face turned pale, wings transparent
brown, and, swiftly, it turned to leave. As did it turn in
flight and meet with the dark ambiance of window pane
a golden light formed about its shivering body,
emanating from the tips of pulsating wings; and in this
golden light it became cocooned, and in the dark glow of
the window pane before it, my bathroom blazed for this
vanquishing light that came crying, ringing, angelic,
defiant, sundering;

how the moth, unaware as I was at the time,
engulfed in a mystified stupor, was to become an
emblem, a motif, of a great light before a reigning
darkness, a light I would chase and in doing so become
transformed; myself resided in the shimmering gaze of
those wings, and how I only knew then, and would only
know for some time, the great lights and darkness,
terrors and beauties, fear and courage of a strange world;
but so it was to be; and so my delusive drama would go
on dictating to the little self that I was; lo! the joy that
comes to he that tries, fails, yet ever tries, and in doing
conquers. Lo! it is to Him in he, by divine grace, having
thou flown through the door between the eyes, that all is
revealed, and each terror, each beauty, becomes realised:

nothing more than mere spectral beams of an incipient dream.

I have done my best here to describe to you that which seems incomprehensible; the commingled beauty and terror of my first encounter with his flesh, The Man That Alludes, or—as we shall call him by—Antwel, and 'his flesh', if *his* flesh you feel yet we can call it, as truly it were mine. But there is no beauty to the way our encounter ends. For, after the feeling of peace and tranquility had dispersed and my stupor evaporated like a steadily thinned mist—following the disappearance of that strange moth creature and the dark glow of Antwel's departing light—reality returned steadily to an utmost normality in my house, and I found myself unable to sleep for the pain that I then endured. How I so ached that night from the fall in the woods, how the pain only then chose to assail my limbs.

So serious and crippling did the pain become, maddening even, that I knew, without much haste, I would pass out. And pass out I did, but alas! it would be untrue to say that my falling unconscious from agony that night spared me the suffering of a nervous and fearing mind;

for in dreams I relived a hundred times my encounter in the mirror with he; I fell again and again from the great height of that dark and windy place in the trees, saw my body, unconscious, twisted and broken in a sea of shadows, fell petrified by moonlight, became again and again humbled in the golden glow of the Moth and the beating of its glorious wings; and, in-between each sliding frame of dream, Antwel appeared to me, and he spoke, and he said to me, silently, through the very lips that were mine:

'Tomorrow, tomorrow you will die.'

'THE MAN THAT ALLUDES', COMING
LATE 2019...

ABOUT THE AUTHOR

Antwel T. Higgins hails from West Yorkshire, where he lives quite happily with his mother and two dogs. His genres are Cosmic-Horror and Cosmic-Fantasy. He studied Literature and Creative Writing at university in York. His pseudonym is an anagram;—can you figure it out? _ _ _ _ _ _ _ _ _ _ _ _ _ _ _ _ _ _ _ _